MW01152530

Taken by the Vampire King

Baton Rouge Vampire: Book 1

Roxie Ray & Lindsey Devin

© 2021

Disclaimer

Contents

Chapter 1 - Leia

The light above me flickered and I glanced toward the ceiling, squinting at it like I could diagnose the issue from a mere irritated gaze and willpower alone. But we were lucky the lights were still on at all, with the stack of red bills clamoring for my attention on my desk, and I sighed as I leaned over the table to swipe my rag over the worn wood.

"Quiet tonight, cher." Harry Allard's soft voice broke the silence, and I stiffened, pausing my movement for just a fraction of a moment.

I shrugged, trying to appear casual. "Guess that's what I get for having ancestors who missed the memo on the direction Baton Rouge would expand in." We weren't exactly on the tourist trail of town, and The Pour House stayed quiet more nights than not. Passing trade had all but been reduced to an army of frogs and too many mosquitoes.

Pierre, Harry's brother, chuckled. "The chicken wings were good tonight, though." He patted his slightly rounded belly, a smile of contentment softening his craggy features.

Pierre wore his ex-police years in the lines and wrinkles of his face like a badge of honor, but he was soft when it came to me—both brothers were, the uncles I'd never had—and Pierre probably contributed the majority of my profits on nights when I served wings.

I nodded, already automatically doing the mental calculations to work out when those would be on the menu again. Takings had probably been good enough to allow more food to be on offer tomorrow. It was always a tussle over paying a bill and trying to earn more money. Speculating to accumulate… But the only thing I fucking seemed to accumulate was more of Dad's gambling debt.

"One day," I said, "life will be better, and I'll have the money to pay all the bills when they need paying, right?" I grinned in the direction of the brothers, their once blond hair now shining more gray under my dim lights.

They were my most loyal regular customers. Always in the same corner like a pair of personal bodyguards. That they were both ex-police definitely helped keep trouble away from my place, too. Their tattoos were as intimidating as their quiet presence for the wrong people, that was for sure.

Well, maybe they couldn't keep the kind of trouble that answered to the name of *Dad* at bay, but not many others tried anything.

Harry nodded. "Hope so, cher." He cleared his throat and shifted in the booth, his bulky frame not quite as much muscle now as it must have been in his youth. "How are things going with…all that?"

He gestured rather than get specific with his words, which gave me the option to not really answer his question, but what the hell? Avoiding the answer didn't make my problems with cashflow any less real.

Things weren't good, and both Harry and Pierre already knew that.

"The same. I'm surrounded by threats of foreclosure and demands for money, and I don't see any of that changing soon." I hesitated as I grabbed a pair of dirty glasses from the end of the bar. "Well, I guess until I'm not surrounded by foreclosure letters and everything is just *gone* instead, right? That would be a change."

As much as the constant threat of losing both the bar and my home loomed over me right now, *actually* losing them both was going to be so much worse. Pierre made a sympathetic noise, but I tuned him out as I took the glasses to the sink before returning to wiping the surfaces. I couldn't afford to start feeling sorry for myself or to accept responsibility for soothing anyone else's sadness.

I just had to get by day to day with a heart that fractured a little more each time I remembered I was on the verge of losing everything—so much family history and the last connection I had to Mom. She'd worked so hard on building the bar before she died, and she wouldn't even recognize it now.

I'd failed her legacy somewhere along the line, and I wouldn't even get a chance to make that right if the bank took everything away. I paused my long sweeps of the counter, ignoring the patches where the varnish lifted and the scarred wood dipped and warped, and I glanced across the room.

This was my kingdom. I reigned here. The jewel-colored bottles on the shelves behind me were among my greatest treasures, and the stale beer odor that lingered here like perfume at all hours of the day and night simply smelled like home.

I'd invested so much of my life into this business—at the expense of making friends and boyfriends, or having any kind of personal life at all. I always had things to do. Tables to clean, order sheets to complete, bill roulette to play. *Which utility company will get lucky this month?* It was truly up to a wildly spinning chamber and fate.

Pierre exhaled a small sigh and stood, his gut hanging just a little over his belt. He drew a creased handkerchief from his pocket and mopped his glistening forehead. "I know you have your reasons, Leia, but damn, it gets hot in here when you turn off that AC."

I grinned in reply. I turned the AC off every evening after the last actual customer had left. Harry and Pierre were welcome to stay as long as they liked—or as long as they could stand to swelter.

"I'm glad you cracked first." His brother chuckled. "We'll see you tomorrow, cher." He offered me a brief hug.

Losing this place would be as tough on them as it would be on me. They'd been friends with Mom and Dad for many years, and The Pour House was pretty much their second home. Not to mention the fact they'd also more or less adopted me when it was clear Dad wasn't up to the role biology had gifted him with.

"Thanks, guys. See you tomorrow." I followed them to the exit and saw them out into the dark night before closing the door against the shadows and twisting the lock.

Then I blew out a sigh as I took the last empty glasses through to the kitchen and left them by the sink. I'd clean them in the morning. It wasn't like they'd run away overnight or I'd have a fairy godmother appear and twitch her nose or whatever. It would be just my luck to have a sudden problem with overfriendly mice, though.

Like I didn't have enough issues without adding pest control to my list of debts.

I trudged through the kitchen—old but clean—
to the tiny back office where I could barely see my
desk. One day I'd tidy this small space, but *sorry
office, today is not your day.*

I sighed. Tomorrow wasn't looking good either
when I considered how many tasks were prioritized
above tidying the office. The atmosphere was
different in here, though. Like something had
moved or *been* moved. I just couldn't quite put my
finger on it.

I glanced at the safe in the corner, every sense
tingling. Forget tingling. My body was blaring an
alarm. Nothing looked disturbed, but there was a
hint of the bourbon Dad favored spicing the air.

That old bastard. He was the reason I changed
the safe combination every week—often enough
that I was in danger of not getting back into it
myself one day, it was so hard to keep them
straight—just so he wouldn't be able to open it and
borrow the takings.

Because it was never stealing in his eyes. It was borrowing, or more likely *investing*.

But not this time.

For fuck's sake. I kneeled down on the old, threadbare carpet—held together only by dust and the power of persuasion—and keyed in the latest combination. I closed my eyes. Dammit. How long had I been using these numbers? Long enough that typing them in was muscle memory, anyway. Shit.

I'd been so distracted by mounting bills, I hadn't changed it on my usual schedule, and Dad had watched me empty the takings last week. Fuck. His beady little gambler's eyes missed nothing at all.

And now, I was missing everything. Where there should have been a neat but small stack of green, there was only the bottom of the safe.

I leaned my back against the wall and rolled my head as I looked consideringly into the empty safe. Well, fuck. Fuckity fuck, fuck, fuck. I would have liked to have an actual coherent thought, but all I had was curse words and a slow buzz of panic that was gradually building to something larger and far more destructive.

One single tear escaped the corner of my eye, and I brushed it away impatiently. Like every other moment, I couldn't give in to sorrow just now or I'd start crying and keep going all night. Harry and Pierre would find me as a dehydrated husk tomorrow.

Too many things ran through my head. Pierre would be disappointed with the lack of chicken wings on the menu tomorrow, but I couldn't even afford a chicken feather right now, never mind a full wing. Of course, the rest of the customers would probably be more disappointed when the beer taps ran dry, but I couldn't even prevent *that*.

Still, what did any of that matter when I couldn't afford the rest of the bills anyway? I'd raised money through so many loans over the years, always desperate to retain the deeds to what was ours, avoiding remortgage in case we lost the house and bar in various attempts to keep us afloat, but now my lines of credit had stretched so thin I could no longer see them.

I had nowhere left to turn, no more tricks left to try.

Soul-deep panic numbed me and made everything feel eons away as I looked around the office. I had paperwork piled up from years before, and red bills littered my desk. Nausea started a slow roll in my gut.

Powerless. I'd never truly experienced having *nothing* left before. But this office, The Pour House, was little more than a mirage now. It would be gone soon enough.

And I'd tried so fucking hard to hang on to all of it.

I'd failed. And that hurt.

I still hadn't moved when there was a shadow at the doorway and Dad stumbled into view, an oversized shot clutched in one hand. For a moment, I wanted to give in to the old hopefulness

I used to have when I saw him—like he might suddenly have realigned his moral compass.

But I knew better than that these days.

"Not content with taking the profits? Drinking them too now?" My voice was hard but without real emotion. There wasn't a day Dad hadn't drunk at least part of our profits.

Today was no different simply because he'd stolen the takings, too.

"I had a tip on a Saints game." His eyes were bleary and unfocused when they met mine, and he slurred his words.

The slurring was bad. He was never a bad tempered drunk. But he was a remorseful one.

And the exaggerated slurring today meant he was particularly remorseful.

I rolled my head toward him, and he watched me warily. Yeah, that was right. He needed to be wary.

"You had a tip?" I kept my voice light as I stood. "Another good tip?"

He shrugged but avoided my gaze. "Turned out not so good."

"I bet." I could barely stand to look at him. He wore his weakness like an ID badge these days, and it was a source of my shame that the biggest reason Pierre and Harry spent so much time protecting me was because they knew Dad couldn't.

They never spoke of it, but we were all aware why they spent so much of their time quietly guarding my business.

"I needed the money. It would have made all of our problems go away." Dad reached toward me, his eyes pleading for my understanding, but I moved away.

"No, Dad. Just fucking no."

His eyes widened.

"What do you think you've done to our problems now? How do you think we'll manage when there's more alcohol in your piss than there is behind the bar?" I could barely contain my anger behind my clipped words and stiff movements.

Dad slumped into the chair behind my desk and it creaked ominously under the sudden weight. The drawer he pulled open groaned in protest, too.

"What are you doing now?" The last thing I needed was him to start interfering in my paperwork.

"My book of contacts." He mumbled the words, and the image of his well-thumbed, black leather notepad came to mind.

When I'd been a child and Dad had been full of smiles and reassurances, I'd loved to see that book in his hands because it always heralded the appearance of one fun friend or another. That was when I'd thought Dad ruled the world. Back before Mom died and Dad became something else. Before he became *this*.

I sighed and shook my head. I never thought about those early childhood days anymore. I could barely remember them and they were as far removed from the present as rainbow unicorns and fairytale castles. I'd taken responsibility for Dad's descent into ruin for so long that I'd stopped believing my Prince Charming might arrive and rescue me. Or any kind of royalty, come to that. But lower-level noblemen tended to avoid me, too.

Now, though, if I saw even so much as a hint of a crown and a royal monogram, or a knight on any kind of white steed coming, I'd lock the door anyway. I had nothing to offer any man—I hadn't even finished high school because I'd spent too many days covering for Dad, nursing Dad, being Dad via email to keep the business running.

Plus, I had no experience of any sort to offer any man. Being a twenty-eight-year-old virgin didn't really *bother* me. After all, some shit people just hadn't time to do yet—and having sex was vying with cleaning the office for priority on my life's to-do list. That said, virginity wasn't exactly a selling point these days. I was practically elderly at this point—and every day that passed made me less confident it was truly a good quality. Society was long past days of purity, after all—experience was definitely where it was at now. At my age, anyway.

Some days—on very *rare* days, when I had the time to spare—I wished I was like any other woman my age, with the ability to be carefree, maybe even a little sexy. Attractive. Desirable. I hadn't walked that walk yet, and I missed something I'd never had.

Dad was still fumbling around in the drawer, and I snapped my focus back to him. "Your *contacts?*" I spat the word. "What the hell good can your bookmaker do for you now? You've spent all the money, Dad. What you haven't gambled, you've tipped down your throat. You're literally pissing it away."

He flinched but didn't look at me as he continued to scrabble through the contents of the drawer. I shrugged as I watched him. What the hell did it matter if he ruined my filing system? We were ruined anyway.

He'd already made sure of that.

"I can't be here with you right now." I pinched the bridge of my nose and inhaled a shaky breath, trying to contain the tears that suddenly prickled behind my eyelids. Frustration rose through me but I expelled it as despair. "Look what you've done to us, Dad! We've got nothing left. You've taken it all, and I… I can't fix this."

The words left me empty, and I dug around in my pocket for my last few dollars and some change. Eight dollars and sixty-three cents. And it was all I had left in the world. I peeled the five-dollar bill off the top and left it on the corner of the desk. Dad looked up from where he was flipping through the pages of the notebook he'd found. He'd been lingering on each page like he needed to wait for his eyes to focus before he read the words.

He met my gaze briefly. "What's that for?"

"Your ride home, Dad. I can't do this with you tonight. I have nothing else in me. I can't take care of anything anymore." Exhaustion rang in my tone. I was bone tired and *so* weary.

Dad returned his attention to the finely lined pages. "I'll take care of it," he murmured.

***

I drove home almost in a daze. On autopilot. Not even enjoying the view of the Spanish moss draped over the live oak trees as I neared our home. Instead, tonight, even through the darkness, every flaw and crack in the paintwork of our house screamed out loud and proud. I knew exactly which rotten boards to avoid on the old front porch, and the way the water pipes clanked and rattled as I filled my bath was familiar even as it scraped over each of my nerves.

Dilapidation. Disrepair.

Bordering on fucking ruin.

"Oh, Mom." The sigh of regret slipped from my lips as I slid into a bath that was barely warm.

Once we'd had a house full of staff and lush gardens that spread out to the edges of a bayou. The crepe myrtles had been magnificent then, rather than twisted and overgrown as they were now. Try as I might, some of the maintenance work always slipped to the bottom of my list. Yard work was usually at the bottom.

Top of my to-do checklist was always Dad. Keeping him barely functioning was second nature. Then I had to keep The Pour House running to ensure we had a little money coming in as well as upholding Mom's legacy. Lastly, I cooked and did laundry, and that was pretty much it. Housework, yardwork, repairs. They just didn't happen. Either the issues resolved themselves or I learned to ignore them.

I lay perfectly still in the rapidly cooling bath water until my stomach rumbled. I wasn't even part way close to relaxed, but I climbed out before dressing and heading to the kitchen. On my way through the house, I passed my floor to ceiling bookcases and trailed my fingers over the books, but I had no desire to select one. Nothing could offer me an escape from reality today—not books and especially not TV. We'd lost cable last month after one overdue bill too many, and now my TV sat dark and silent in the corner like some sort of postmodern ornament. I was pretty sure it was judging me, actually.

I was certainly judging me.

And the judgement didn't stop when I practically hung inside the fridge, gazing over the empty shelves like something edible might magically appear.

I dug my hand into my pocket again, pulling out my remaining three dollars and sixty-three cents.

It wouldn't buy me a lot, but I should be able to get some pasta and the vegetables to make a sauce. Dad would probably be hungry when he got home as well. I was too angry with him to really take him into consideration this evening, but I did it automatically.

Even though he didn't deserve it.

I sighed as I grabbed my keys and walked back to my car. Working at the bar meant I kept the antisocial hours of a vampire, but at least the grocery store would be quiet.

I zipped around the store, familiar with all the aisles and the bargain areas, then paid for my purchases and left before shame ate me up at the meager selection I could afford. That shame burned within me stronger than any hunger. I stuck to the lit walkway as I returned to my car, although the low purr of an engine idling nearby alerted me to a limo at the curb. I paused for a moment because… hell, an actual *limo*, so dark in the back I couldn't see who was in there, even with the window partly open.

A limo. I didn't think people who rode in those even knew this part of town existed.

I walked by, forcing myself forward even as my legs slowed, feet hesitating to take the next step. Dammit. I had too much else to worry about to be curious about the owner of a way too expensive car in a cheap grocery store parking lot.

But a strange desire to *know* ripped through me, accompanied by a different sort of desire. The sort that whispered of the company of another on sweaty night, full of heat and touch and rumpled bed sheets.

I shivered as my body beat a sudden pulse of awareness, and hurried past the parked car. But I turned at the soft *clunk* of a car door closing behind me, and my throat dried as I gazed at the tall guy now standing by the limo. His hair was longer on top, and tousled, and the lights revealed an angular jawline and turbulent gray eyes that glittered with interest as his lips quirked in a slow, easy smile.

I parted my lips to speak but no words came out as he sauntered toward me, and I remained fixed in place, just watching him get closer. Part of me wanted to turn and run away like he was some kind of predator, but the other part of me wanted to…

Shit. I didn't know what I wanted to do. Watch him? Drink him in? Welcome him somehow? My body tingled like it knew exactly what kind of welcome to offer.

I backed up until my ass bumped against the brick wall behind me, and my small bag of groceries fell from my hand as the man's gaze remained fixed on mine, incredibly intense.

Something about him…

I shook my head, not sure where my tangled thoughts were leading. Then suddenly he stood in front of me, his fingers toying with the ends of my brown hair, and I lifted my chin to look up at him as he surrounded me like a shadow, his presence commanding, his scent masculine spice and exciting.

The first real touch was a light caress of his knuckles down my cheek. I closed my eyes, savoring something so unexpected and fleeting, melting into a spell meant only for me.

Then I jerked back at his soft mouth on mine, my head striking the wall before I relaxed and inhaled a breath of longing that allowed his tongue to slide past my lips—quiet, casual, exploring. He stroked the inside of my mouth before wrapping his arms around me and urging me closer to him as he groaned in a way I'd never heard. Somewhere between longing and satisfaction.

The tips of my fingers touched his cheek before I pushed them into his hair, gripping onto him as he controlled my mouth and pleasure twisted a slow spiral through me in a physical response I'd never experienced with anyone.

I sucked breath after quick breath, my breathing lost all rhythm and coordination, and I grew light-headed as I tried to answer the persuasion and teasing of his lips and tongue. My heart thundered in my chest, and my nipples hardened where they pressed against him. I'd never wanted a man more, and the thought rippled through my head in a blaze of desire and wantonness as I ground against his thigh.

When he released me, he rested his forehead against mine and sucked in deep breaths as his chest rose and fell before he dropped his head so his mouth hovered over my neck. As my heart beat faster, the pulse below his mouth turned suddenly wild, like something was trapped beneath my skin. I could feel it—as though it was answering some kind of call to make itself known.

Holy crap... This was... It was incredible.

Wait. No. It was actually *insane*. This guy was a complete stranger, and here I was, making out with him on the street?!

What the hell was I *doing*?

I shoved him. Before I even thought about it, I thrust my hands against the stranger's chest, and his mouth gaped as his eyes widened and he staggered back, leaving just enough space for me to run.

My chest ached with every breath I sucked in, and I couldn't hear anything but the blood pounding through my ears as I focused on my feet striking the sidewalk, running back into the store. Adrenaline fueled my panic. Fear tightened all of my muscles, but there was also something else. A fascination and enjoyment I couldn't hide from. Desire still coiled low in my body.

The limo was gone when I eventually left the store again, but my small bag of groceries sat on the curb like it was waiting for a ride, and after I'd collected it, my hands trembled all the way home.

Chapter 2 – Nic

Fuck. Yesterday, I'd held the very thing that would complete my full ascension to my father's throne in my arms—and I'd watched her run away. It wasn't like I could chase her down the sidewalk, though. People frowned on that kind of thing these days.

I sighed. It shouldn't be too hard to find that specific virgin again, though. It wasn't like the world was teeming with them anymore. And none had ever affected me quite like the brunette with the startling green eyes. Her scent alone... nothing screamed *virgin* quite like it.

In fact, something screamed *mine*.

I made it a habit to stay far away from humans. Fucking *humans*. But the virgin issue... I'd hoped to put it off for longer. Hadn't even really been looking. Mother was more anxious than I was, wanting me to make my final ascension to the throne. I was king in name—the rightful heir, but open to challenge before I claimed a pure woman...or something like that. I thought it all rather ridiculous, even though I knew I'd follow through on the lore one day, if only to cement my claim to the throne in the eyes of my people.

But Mother believed in all the old lore—the pent-up sexual energy of a virgin, the burst of power it would offer me, and the longevity her blood would grant. There were all kinds of rules I could only half-remember. Virginity had to be offered willingly—the energy would only work if freely given and couldn't be taken by force.

I wasn't so sure. None of what Mother said seemed to work with the modern world anymore... And the stuff about true mates? I'd always imagined it to be fairytales, something to hope for but not to expect...

But fuck, that *kiss*.

I stood in my closet, surrounded by the clothing that defined my entire image. All the shades of black. I selected a shirt—wrinkle free, of course—and a jacket to match my pants as I ignored yesterday's shirt, carefully arranged on a hanger and hooked over one of the small door handles that opened individual cupboards for me to peruse ties or shoes.

Every now and then, I tortured myself by wandering closer to that shirt, by inhaling until I filled my chest with the most tantalizing scent I'd ever fucking inhaled.

My cock jerked in my pants as I drew the breaths, as I engaged in the sweet torture of closing my eyes and allowing my nose to linger close to the fabric, stirring the memories of the woman I'd wrapped in my arms…at least until she pushed me away, forcing me to return to my senses and reclaim my control.

I'd been moments away from thrusting into her on the sidewalk and claiming her as mine.

I palmed my cock as it twitched again at the memory of the woman I'd allowed to run. I'd been on my way to a meeting when I detected her scent, like a siren call meant only for me, and I'd made Jenkins pull over.

But I hadn't meant to get out of the car. Or approach her.

Or fucking kiss her.

Because now I couldn't stop thinking about her.

And that wouldn't do. I knew how to control myself at all times.

Only I hadn't controlled myself outside that grocery store. I'd run on instinct. Centuries old instinct I'd never even known existed. Or I hadn't believed in it anyway.

Something else lurked below that kiss. Something other than merely *virgin*.

My cock swelled further under my touch, and I swallowed a groan. I'd already taken myself in hand to thoughts of the woman when I got home last night... Then in the shower this morning... And now I hungered for her again.

But I glanced at my watch. My body would have to wait for relief and release. I had a meeting at work I couldn't be late for. And today I would channel all of my frustration into making people *pay*.

I grabbed my jacket and shoved my arms into the sleeves then strode through the door—but not before I breathed in deeply by that damn shirt again. I'd never been so fucking tempted.

And I resented the temptation, because it brought a whole new set of problems to my door. I didn't spend my time with humans. And I certainly didn't run around kissing them like my soul would catch fire if I didn't.

***

I glanced around the meeting room at La Petite Mort and inhaled the mix of greed, lust and loss of control that seeped in from the casino beyond the closed door. The casino floor remained within my view through the giant one-way mirror that looked out over the main game room.

Even though it was still early in the day, tables were occupied, my dealers were busy, customers were drinking, and most were losing their money.

Yes, the day already smelled like success.

Success and one fucking human virgin who seemed to have invaded my actual blood.

"Benedict." I looked at my best friend and the man I trusted with all aspects of my life. "Have you prepared the list?"

Something about calling debts in today appealed to my sense of control. The house always won, after all. And it was a good outlet for my frustration. Something else to focus on so I didn't have to consider the family battle my discovery of such a tantalizing virgin might ignite.

Benedict grimaced and slid five buff-colored files of paperwork across the table between us. "Each of these individuals owes more than one-hundred thousand dollars. One of them owes very much more than that."

Jason, my bodyguard, whistled then held his hands up when I glanced at him. "Seems like a lot to let get away, that's all."

I grinned, sure it wasn't a pleasant expression. "That's why I'm not."

A ripple of laughter ran around the table as members of my staff sought to ingratiate themselves with me.

"I think you'll definitely find the top one most fascinating of all. It's the one with the most debt, but also the most interesting things to call in." Benedict tapped it with the end of his pen. "And he's been calling to try to extend his line of credit."

"Really?" I raised an eyebrow and flipped the folder open.

It all looked fairly standard, and I murmured aloud as I perused the usual conditions.

"He put his bar up as collateral—among other things. Check the most recent sub-clause." There was amusement in Benedict's voice.

I stiffened. "His bar?" Suddenly I spoke through fangs that threatened to descend to their full length as the details behind the file came into sharp focus and the first flickers of anger claimed me.

"Yes." Benedict wasn't bothered by my sudden display of temper, but some of my other staff shrank away. "And like I said, he's been calling on the phone since yesterday. Obviously got himself into some more...difficulties."

"Fucking humans." My voice was a low growl.

But Benedict laughed. "I thought you didn't believe in that?"

And just like that, my mind was immediately back with the woman from outside the store, and my dick twitched. But I swallowed down the sudden whisper of desire and recalled my anger before setting Jean Boucher's file to one side while Benedict talked me through the other collections cases.

I glanced back at the Boucher file for the rest of the morning, though. Stupid fucking drunk. Only reason I gave him a tab in the first place was because I'd known his family a long time. Well, his wife's family. Boucher had walked into a sweet setup of a marriage with the daughter of one of Baton Rouge's oldest families.

A family I'd known since the beginning here, and a bar I'd frequented nearly as long throughout the decades. I'd watched over every generation of that family, and it had only taken one drunk man with a weakness for giving his money away to bring everything tumbling around his ears.

It seemed he'd built his newest house with *my* cards, and I was about to bring it all toppling down.

Guilt gnawed at me, though. I'd lost touch with the family around the time of Camille's marriage to Jean, too caught up with Father's descent into his long, slow demise and my inevitable rise to the throne to bother with the only humans I seemed capable of tolerating. Even their presence had irritated me at the time, so I'd cut all ties and focused on my future role, doing my best to prepare and forge the alliances that would sustain me through my transition from heir to king.

Regret was a useless emotion, but I sighed as I stood and walked to the window, looking out over the humans who couldn't see me, the ones who might get lucky every now and again, but who would ultimately lose. Because I wanted to win. I controlled their every moment in here. There were no clocks, so they wasted hours of daylight, never aware when sunset passed to night or sunrise to day. The seats were just comfortable enough to relax into before the play at another table attracted their attention, and the high-stakes slots in another room played a celebratory tune no matter the size of the win.

Here, these humans were mine.

Only now, what Jean Boucher had was also mine. He might as well have gift wrapped it with a bow and presented it to me.

I rested my fist briefly on the glass. I'd long since become immune to the stupidity of humans, how they always reached in vain for the unattainable, but every now and again one of them surprised me with the extent of their belief that they would triumph despite the odds.

And in this particular case, I couldn't help but feel sympathy for the long line of family members I'd watched toil to build their small but worthy Baton Rouge empire—an empire that only took the mistakes of one man to crush. They kind of felt like my family, in some odd and remote way, and it would please me to watch Jean Boucher pay for his fucking stupidity.

Guilt at neglecting them for so long washed through me again, but that kind of sentimentality was ridiculous. Humans meant nothing to me, and Father's decline had needed to be hidden for as long as possible. It had taken all of my attention.

But I would make Jean pay now. It would help work out some of my frustration if nothing else.

"Nic?" Benedict's tone suggested this wasn't the first time he'd spoken my name as a question.

"Yes?" I threw the terse reply over my shoulder, barely even glancing behind me.

"I asked if you'd seen the sub-clause I mentioned." My friend sounded like this particularly interested him, but anger over the fact that it just took one dumbfuck in a long line of decent people to screw up a good thing still caused tension in my muscles.

The plantation home and bar Jean Boucher had gambled away had been in Baton Rouge nearly as long as I had, and I'd always taken a little comfort in knowing they were both here unchanged. An immortal life was a long one with many changes, and I'd taken my comfort in a constant.

I grinned ruefully. That probably made *me* the dumbfuck.

"I remember the sub-clause." I turned away from watching the people gambling their lives away. Gambling their lives to me.

"Doesn't it interest you?" Benedict quirked his eyebrow, but I shrugged.

"Not particularly. What's an extra piece of collateral wagered by a drunkard?" I took my seat and flipped through the paperwork again. The outstanding amount on his tab probably didn't even reflect what he'd poured into La Petite Mort over the years.

When he'd stopped having free cash to plow into his habit, he'd turned to credit. To his house. To his bar. To other valuable things.

"I'll collect this debt myself." I shoved the file from me, disgust at Boucher making my movements sharp.

"You?" There went Benedict's fucking eyebrow quirking again, and with good reason.

My entire staff was well aware of my thinly concealed intolerance of humans, but I needed to do *something* that wasn't demanded of a new king. I wanted to just be a casino owner again, needed some *action*.

But being a casino owner didn't negate the fact that I was now king, and I'd spoken, and Benedict had dared question me, so I glared at him. And at every other fucker at the table for good measure. They all dropped their gazes, suddenly busy with other files. *Any* other files.

"What do you need me to do?" Jason asked. He was the only one I didn't scare, which was endearing when I was in a good mood and frustrating when I wasn't. But beyond being my bodyguard, he was also my sireling, and he never had anything to fear from me because that bond between us was strong.

"Get legal to draw up the paperwork we require to call in Boucher's debts. *All* of his debts." I passed the file to Jason so he'd be able to follow my instructions.

He tucked it under his arm and slid his phone from his pocket. "I'll call them now."

"No."

He looked at me.

"No. You go there, and you fucking stand over them. Make yourself at home in their office. We do this today." I watched Jason until he all but saluted.

I needed this win today, this *control*, to take my mind off the human woman. I couldn't dedicate time to finding her today, so I needed something else to focus on. I'd find her later, though. Find her and explore all of the delicious opportunities her scent offered, so fucking help me.

A human. I could hardly stand to think about it, even though I'd known this day would come if my mother was correct in her superstitions. It wasn't like virgin vampires still existed.

"Let me know when you've got the paperwork. Benedict, I'll leave you to handle the rest of these files."

Benedict nodded as I left the room and strode to my office. Jason was already on his phone, warning our legal team of his impending arrival.

I grabbed my gun from my safe and secured it in the shoulder holster under my suit jacket. Technically, I absolutely didn't need a gun. I was quite capable of... I grinned... *neutralizing any threat* without the use of firearms. However, and also on a technicality, I absolutely needed the gun. I couldn't reveal myself as vampire to humans because we weren't supposed to actually exist, never mind roam among them. We pretty much all obeyed the creed—even the newly turned ones. And those who didn't... Well, we dealt with them. Just not with guns.

Still, I was seeing humans today, and sometimes a gun was the only way to scare them. It was what they understood.

Although usually my natural charm was scary enough on its own.

Jason knocked on my door very quickly with the contracts I needed, and soon I was in my limo and heading to Jean Boucher's plantation property just outside town. I remained quiet as we sped along, my mind alternating between the task at hand and the woman from last night. Desire flared through me again, but I restrained it by refocusing on the contract, reading it over, preparing for all the arguments Boucher would likely have.

He didn't deserve to keep the properties his wife's family had worked so hard to establish and maintain. They were both better off with me. I couldn't do anything else for Camille and her ancestors, but maybe I could rescue what Jean had ruined.

The stores and concrete soon gave way to open land and trees. It was boggy out here but the Boucher house was in a nice area, and I could probably make it quite useful or lucrative. I could even open a second casino location or a boutique hotel, perhaps.

But when Jenkins, my driver, swung into a heavily pot-holed driveway, driving between cracked and leaning gateposts, complete with wrought iron gates hanging lazily from their hinges, I sat up a little straighter, eager for my first glimpse of the house beyond the overgrown bushes and shrubs.

Spanish moss hung from the trees like tangled hair instead of graceful curtains, giving the impression that this place was no longer worth what Jean Boucher had led me to believe.

By calling in his debt, I was inviting all kinds of further financial problems.

I cleared my throat, and Jenkins half-glanced over his shoulder.

"Yes, sir?"

I shifted in my seat, leaning forward, and rolled down my window. "You know, maybe we should just turn arou—"

The main house came into view and a tantalizing, familiar scent drifted into the car. The scent of a viable, of-age virgin. But surely two in Baton Rouge in as many days was too much of a coincidence? I wouldn't have remained oblivious to *two* of them, surely? And especially two that made my dick stand up and take notice like this.

"Sorry, sir?"

I shook my head. Maybe virgins were like buses. You waited for one for ages and then two came along at once. "You know what? Nothing. I shouldn't think I'll be very long here. You can just wait outside."

Now, I'd only come here for one thing. But there appeared to be a virgin inside who belonged to me, unless my nose was playing tricks on me.

"Very good, sir." He rolled smoothly to a stop in a driveway overgrown with weeds, and when I stepped from the car, I let my gaze wander up the building. More weeds sprouted from the steps at the front, and some sort of creeper plant covered the side of the building and had invaded its way under the roof tiles.

I shook my head. "For fuck's sake." This looked increasingly like a bad idea, but a contract was a contract, and I owed this to Camille's line. Her family line of women had always been particularly strong. Special, almost.

I approached the front door, stepping over rotten boards as I went. No one answered the knock on the door, but when I twisted the handle, it swung open to reveal a dark entrance hall. Dust motes hung in a thin stream of light seeping from around the edges of heavy velvet curtains.

"Hello?" My voice echoed in the vast space. Had Boucher gambled away every stick of furniture, too? His wife should have nailed things down before her passing.

I drew a deep breath—a prelude to a sigh—then stopped as my head spun. That woman. She was definitely here. Her scent filled my nose, and I almost groaned as I took another breath. She was here somewhere, and…shit. It was like she'd put a spell on me. More than simply being a virgin, every fiber of my being raged that she was meant for me.

I steadied myself on the doorframe before looking at the folder in my hand, trying to remember what the hell I was doing.

"Hello?" I called again, and a muffled groan answered me from beyond the closest doorway. I followed the noise and found a man sitting on a sofa, his head in his hands.

"Jean Boucher?" I phrased his name like a question, but of course it was fucking him. I'd observed him in La Petite Mort often enough.

He looked up, and his eyes widened. His face paled and he covered his mouth with his hand. "I didn't think you'd come."

He inched away from me until he was almost at the edge of the chaise, and fear radiated from him, turning the air in the room thick and cloying.

I moved aside some dirty glasses on a low coffee table and set the paperwork down so he could see it. He swayed a little and his face paled further.

"What's going on?" A voice spoke from the doorway, and I didn't even need to turn to know it was the woman whose scent seemed to have become part of my DNA, however impossible.

"I... I called Nicolas. This is Nicolas Dupont. We need his help." Boucher's voice was shaky, but I shook my head.

I hadn't gotten those messages, beyond Benedict's brief mentions. "That's not why I'm here."

Boucher tried again. "There are some things I need to explain, Leia." His eyes pleaded with the woman I still hadn't looked at, and I held myself stiff as I tried not to glance at her. "I've made a mistake," he whispered.

"You've made a lot of fucking *big* mistakes, Dad," Leia—her name was *Leia*—said. "But what have you done this time?"

"I used the house." Boucher closed his eyes and groaned. "I used the house and the bar as collateral. I wanted... I wanted Mr. Dupont to extend my line of credit, but it looks like he's come to call in my debt instead."

I nodded then clucked my tongue and shook my head slowly. "Ah, Jean," I said, trying to look as though I was considering a problem when I'd already worked out my next play. "I *have* come to call in what you owe me, but I might have a more favorable solution."

"Anything." He almost reached for me as desperation lit his bloodshot eyes.

I fanned the paperwork over the table, then drew his attention to the relevant subclause. "Do you remember this addition you made?"

He looked at me, his eyes widening as he slowly shook his head. "Not that," he whispered.

I nodded. "Oh yes, you've got something of great value that I'd like very much indeed."

I looked over my shoulder and allowed myself a small smile at Leia's surprise as she met my gaze.

Chapter 3 - Leia

Holy fuck. Those gray eyes, that full mouth. I'd know those lips anywhere. I could still feel them on my own. I lifted my hand and pressed my finger to my mouth briefly as the memory washed over me, and Nicolas Dupont's pupils flared as he watched the movement.

My skin heated as I remembered dreams that had ended with me tangled in my sheets, odd half-thoughts of this man's tongue skating across my skin still echoing in my mind.

But right now, fury overshadowed sexual desire, repressing any crazy urge I'd had to sleep with him. No. *Now*, I wanted to karate chop him to the throat or knee him really hard in the balls.

What the hell, right? The man who'd sent insane awareness and desire whirling through me, stealing my self-control and making me want to forget myself, had just turned up in my home.

Apparently to *take* my home. I shook my head and glanced toward the staircase that had been ornate once upon a time. Maybe I was still asleep. Dreaming. Something.

"Dad?" I didn't do a whole lot hesitantly in my life—taking care of Dad and The Pour House had taught me I had to mean it or no one would take me seriously, but I couldn't help the tentative note in my voice now. "What's going on?"

"Miss Boucher." The man who didn't belong here stood and offered his hand. "I'm Nicolas Dupont."

"So my father said." I folded my arms and narrowed my eyes, even though the French pronunciation he gave his name sent a flutter of excitement through me.

After a moment of awkwardness that I was determined not to make any easier, Nicolas Dupont retracted his hand and sat down, reaching for the paperwork he'd laid out for Dad. "The terms are all in here. Your father has accumulated significant debt at La Petite Mort—"

I gasped. I recognized the name of the casino, but there was something strangely erotic about the phrase on Nicolas Dupont's lips. I wandered to the other side of the room because there was something magnetic about him, and I clearly needed to avoid his pull.

Dad held his head in his hands, not meeting my gaze, and I swallowed against the lump of anxiety lodged in my throat.

"How much, Dad?" My voice came out low, but not because I deliberately pitched it that way. Because fear had seized control of my vocal cords, and it was all I could manage.

Dad shook his head and groaned.

I asked him again, aware of Nicolas's Dupont's gaze on me like he was searing a brand to my skin, but I didn't dare look at him. As many times as I asked Dad how much he owed, I wasn't sure I truly wanted to know.

But the casino owner cleared his throat. "It's a vast amount, far exceeding one-hundred thousand dollars." There was no real sympathy in his hard words. Just statement of fact as my knees weakened and I placed my palm flat on the wall for support as he continued in that same eerie, all-business tone. "These legal documents allow me to take possession of this building—"

"My *home*," I whispered as pain tightened a band around my chest.

"And also a business." He shuffled the paperwork. "The Pour House?"

I met his eyes, and although he'd phrased the name as a question, it wasn't. He knew exactly what the documentation entitled him to, and he wasn't asking my permission.

"There's no way." I forced the words past my lips as I took stiff steps to the nearest chair. "I can't afford to settle those debts."

On top of the bills and mortgage repayments, and the refurbishment that clearly needed doing...

Eye-watering gambling debt. My next inhale caught in my chest, and for a moment, I struggled to release it, like the air I needed to survive could kill me as easily as sustain me.

I shook my head against the truth of what Dad had done this time. Why hadn't I known? Well, this was truly it. No matter what I tried, my efforts to keep us afloat would never be enough.

"Dad." My whisper was a noise of pain and censure. Disappointment and disbelief.

His betrayal was a gut punch. Everything was about to be taken away. Perhaps this was what rock bottom looked like.

"Leia." Dad held his arms out, his eyes pleading. "Just listen. It's all going to be okay. I've been trying to extend my credit. I just need one big win and then I can stop. I can make everything better. I can fix up this place, make it so you don't have to work so hard. You can stop worrying."

"I'll never stop worrying, though, will I?" I hissed the words, too angry to yell. My eyes itched like a bitch as I withheld my tears. Neither of these men deserved to see my sorrow.

"I'll fix it." But Dad wheedled the words like a child, and I'd heard that tone often enough over the years that I knew he was only begging for one more opportunity to screw up.

"I'm done listening, Dad." I held my hand out to emphasize my point and I looked away, not meeting the piercing gaze of Nicolas Dupont, either.

And then traitorous hope reared its head, as it always did. Maybe I was just looking at this all wrong. I didn't need to give up. The battle wasn't lost until I stopped fighting. I curled my hands into fists, tightening them until my knuckles gleamed and strained white against my skin.

"You need to eat."

I turned my attention to the casino owner, the messenger I most definitely wanted to shoot, but he looked as if he hadn't spoken, even though the soft words had been laced with unexpected concern.

"I need to fix this shit, is what I need to do," I said.

Dupont's flicker of a smile was mocking with a touch of indulgence, and irritation flared hot through my veins. I didn't need this guy humoring me. I tensed my jaw and squeezed my fists harder, resting them in my lap.

"I'll fix this by any means necessary," I said. I couldn't just lose everything. I couldn't fucking allow Dad to rip it all away. Everything I'd held on to and built... My thoughts faded to the white noise of static as I met the businessman's eyes. "There must be something I can do."

"Well..." Dupont screwed up his mouth a little like he was considering something. Then he passed the paperwork to Dad. "If I can just draw your attention back to the subclause you just dismissed? A recently added item of collateral, I believe, if you note the date? Make sure you read it carefully."

Dad bent over the paperwork then shifted so a shaft of the dust-mote filled sunlight shone directly on the pages before bringing them closer to his face like he was trying to find the right level of focus.

He made an animal-like noise of grief and his face paled as he turned to look at me.

"What?" My whole body was rigid. "What the fuck did you lose now?"

Surely there was nothing else? Couldn't Nicolas Dupont see he already had everything, that he was literally sitting in the ruins of our lives? I crept around to be closer to them so we could talk this through.

But Dupont just turned toward Dad like they were in the middle of a private negotiation, his broad shoulders—made all the broader by the well-fitting suit that clung to his muscular back—effectively preventing me from participating in the conversation.

His voice rumbled back to me. "If you agree to honor the subclause, I'll forgive everything else."

I exhaled a sudden breath. Well, shit. That was a no brainer. "One subclause and everything else remains ours?" I asked, but neither man looked at me.

Dad simply gazed at our unwanted guest like he alone could save him. Then he nodded. "I agree."

"And what are you agreeing to?" Dupont's voice was quiet and calm, soothing as it wrapped around my thoughts, beguiling me with the idea everything could be fixed.

I didn't damn well care what Dad was agreeing to—he just needed to do it quickly so I could go and start my day's work at the bar. In fact, I was thinking so hard about all the things I needed to do I almost didn't listen as Dad began to speak. Until I heard my name.

"My daughter, Leia. You can have her as stated in the sub-clause of the contract."

I shot to my feet, heart racing. "What now? No. I'm no one's collateral."

But Dupont merely chuckled, never breaking his eye-contact with Dad. "I've accepted stranger things to secure freedom from accumulated debt."

"*Dad.*" His name left my lips as a plea.

He didn't reply.

"Dad!" I tried again, more emphatic this time. "Dad, what have you done?"

He shrugged, his eyes darting to meet mine briefly. "I was drunk. Desperate. I don't remember. But this could fix everything. *You* have the power to fix *everything*, Leia."

I took a deep breath in, aiming for some sort of meditative calm, but I misjudged and filled myself with pure rage instead. "You stupid pair of bastards. No one calls in a woman to settle gambling debt. What about the law? What about sex-trafficking?"

"Oh? Will there be sex?" Dupont's voice was smooth and warm, and I trembled with anger.

"Never. This is about fifty shades of illegal, and you know it. Dad, you can't do this." I wanted to save everything, but not at the expense of *me*. "We've got to try another way. There must be something."

Dad breathed deeply and seemed in control of himself for the first time all morning as he finally met my gaze properly. "No, there isn't, Leia. I'm sorry, but I won't go back on a contract I signed. This might not be the outcome I expected, but it is what it is."

"It is what it *is*?" I fought to keep my voice under control. "That's all you have to say?"

Nicolas shrugged and answered on Dad's behalf. "It's unfortunate, but it's not for very long. You'll be able to return home soon."

That was the first positive thing I'd heard him say, but I wasn't about to let him know that. "Oh really? And am I supposed to be grateful?"

Dupont spoke again. "Your father set a stipulation on your availability when he added you to the contract. A one-month term." He shrugged a second time. "It should be sufficient."

When he glanced over his shoulder at me, his eyes gleamed.

"For what?" I ran my hand over the ornate tapestry arm of the antique sofa. The threads were loose with wear and age, tugging free of their complex woven pattern. I steeled myself for the conversation the three of us were clearly about to have. "Just for the record, I agree to none of this."

Dupont reached toward me and I shifted away. His eyes narrowed, his gaze growing colder. "Miss Boucher."

I nodded at the formality. Good. That was the kind of distance I could get used to. I was over the whole business of his tongue in my mouth. I waved my hand briefly like I could flick away my unwanted thoughts. "I'm listening."

But I was only listening because nothing meant more to me than Mom's family home and the business she'd worked so hard to maintain. I couldn't lose either. For those two things, I would have crawled to Nicolas Dupont's side over broken glass. I couldn't let her memory down. I refused to be the Boucher that ruined it all.

He nodded and kept his gaze trained on me as I shifted uncomfortably under those gray eyes that seemed to flash almost silver at times or darken with the threat of a storm. "I seek a business arrangement."

I nodded but said nothing. I wasn't about to put any words into his mouth.

"I have no need of anything…" His gaze skimmed me as he paused, his pupils dilating so briefly I might have imagined it. "Physical."

I crossed my arms, actively shielding myself from any more lingering gazes.

"I simply need a companion to accompany me to some forthcoming events with my family and my business associates."

"Arm candy?" I hadn't meant to interrupt, but surely I could be no one's first choice for that? My hair was always wash and wear, my clothes were thrift shop finds, and I wore the scent of beer and the sweat of hard work like other women wore perfume.

His lip curled a little. "Arm candy isn't a label I'd use. But this is certainly a business arrangement you'd be quite stupid to refuse. A mere one month of your time to retain everything your father has gambled away to me?"

I glanced beyond him to Dad, who looked broken as he stared unfocused at our cracked fireplace. But looks were deceiving. He'd only look so fragile until he had the bright idea to place another bet or return to the gaming tables at La Petite Mort.

A shiver raced through me, and Dupont's face tightened like my sudden, private fear meant something to him.

And they were both clearly holding back information. Deals like this one didn't exist. But Dad was right about one thing—we were desperate.

"So, it seems you have a choice." Dupont looked as though it took some effort to relax as he addressed me. "I can *either* take everything that's legally mine." He gestured, his one arm wave presumably encompassing the house and even the bar. "Or you simply agree to the sub-clause, a one-month term with me, and you can retain the other collateral. I'd ensure the deeds would be put back in your name, and…" He spared a glance for Dad. "No one could ever gamble them away again."

I struggled not to gape at him, my muscles aching with the strain of holding my mouth closed. "Mine?"

He nodded. "You have the power to fix this."

I waited a beat. "Maybe, but why do I also feel like I don't have much say?"

He gave an elegant shrug, that of a patient man, a predator. "No one is forcing your hand."

"Only offering me everything I've ever wanted while certainly not telling me everything."

He only shrugged again like he was completely unaffected by the turmoil in my head—turmoil *he'd* induced. I exhaled slowly. Maybe I didn't need to be conflicted over this. It wasn't like I was being offered up for sacrifice.

It was a business arrangement with a businessman. Escort to functions, nothing physical, one-month time limit. Put like that, it didn't sound so bad. Especially considering all I stood to gain.

Which was why there *had* to be something else—something I was missing.

But was that missing thing enough to prevent me from saying yes?

I just had to negotiate carefully, that was all. "Okay. And what if I have some conditions of my own?" I pressed my lips closed against a sigh of frustration. I hadn't meant to weaken myself at the start by making my additional demands into a question, something he could refuse.

But he nodded. "I'm willing to listen."

Okay. Okay, if he'd listen, I'd talk. I kept my sigh of relief in my chest. I wanted to look confident and assured.

"First." I ticked it off on my finger then glanced at him to check if he was aware this meant I was actually making a list. "I won't sleep in your bed. I want my own space with guaranteed privacy. Second, I won't do anything degrading or horrible."

He lifted an eyebrow.

"Like wear anything I deem too slutty or kill anyone or something like that," I expanded, waving a hand like this was something I was used to discussing. Negotiations I could do, although they were usually with the brewery or the utility companies.

"Got it. No killing." He sounded faintly amused, but I didn't regret actually stating the no killing condition. If he took women as payment, God only knew what else he was up to.

"Anything further?"

When I nodded, Dupont's jaw tensed briefly before he returned to looking relaxed.

"Two things. I can't be away from The Pour House for a month. It's too long to leave it closed up—there's no point retaining ownership to a business that's gone out of business due to being closed for a month, right? So I want a temporary manager. Someone to oversee it and keep it running while I can't be there. It isn't something I can trust Dad to do."

Dupont nodded. "Done. And the final thing?"

I rolled my eyes. I would have maybe tried to insert another last clause, but it looked like his desire to humor me was wearing thin.

"I want my Dad checked into rehab for his addictions and I want him to be unwelcome in La…in your casino." I couldn't say the name, although his eyes seemed to flicker slightly, like they could burn me, just from the fact I'd even considered it. But I pushed on. "I want him to be *persona non grata* all over Baton Rouge for gambling."

"There are other cities." Dupont dismissed my concern with a quick wave, but I glared at him, and he inclined his head. "But I'll talk with the others in my network, and Jean will no longer be welcome at La Petite Mort." He lingered over the last three words, his mouth and tongue seeming to caress them as he watched me. "Is that all?"

I ran my requests back through my head. "I covered privacy, dress, The Pour House, and Dad, so yeah. That's all."

"Don't forget *no killing*." His eyes gleamed with momentary amusement again, but there was a cold edge, and I shivered under his gaze. "Perfect. Done. I agree to your terms."

He held his hand between us.

"Wait. That was fast. What about negotiations of your own that need addressing? Don't you have anything to add or anything to try to get me to reconsider?" This was way too easy. Something was definitely up.

Dupont tilted his head as he studied me. "Anything particular need further negotiation? Sudden desire to kill someone or to sleep with me?"

Heat flared into my cheeks, and I curved my fingers against the cushions of the sofa. "No."

"Well then." He glanced at his hand, still suspended midair between us, and with reluctance, I took it, wrapping my fingers around his and remembering the way he'd touched me as he kissed me.

More heat flared through my body, scorching the inside of me with awareness before pulsing at my clit. I closed my eyes. There was way more to this *business arrangement* than I knew. There had to be, but there was also no other way to protect everything Mom had worked so hard for—my past and my future.

"Thank you." The words were out of my mouth before I could take them back, and one corner of his lips quirked up.

"I believe I should be thanking you, Miss Boucher."

But I'd already committed, so I continued. "Thank you for giving me the chance to save my home and my bar. It's sort of a legacy. My mother's family has owned both for a very long time, and my maternal family line can be traced back to the settlement of Baton Rouge." I glanced around. "I know it doesn't look like much. It's run down, fallen into disrepair, and Mom would hardly recognize the place now, but one day I'll bring it back to its former glory and make her proud. And you've given me that opportunity back."

I looked quickly at Dad, but he was half-dozing where he sat, certainly not listening, and not the least perturbed at the events he'd set in motion.

For a moment, Dupont was quiet, like I'd surprised him. Then he nodded. "I think sometimes we create our own opportunities. But I'm glad to see family means so much to you." He nodded again, the movement decisive and approving. "I think we'll be just fine this month, Miss Boucher. In fact, I think we might get along very well indeed. You might even be surprised at just *how* well."

Then he smiled, that strange, predatory light back in his eyes as he inhaled so deeply his chest broadened, and too many emotions took root in me. Apprehension, confusion, excitement, fear, and desire all warred under my skin.

What the hell had I just done?

Chapter 4 - Nic

"Miss Boucher?" Even suspicion looked good on her, the way she narrowed her eyes when I referred to her formally, handing her the distance she so clearly craved but didn't seem to believe in.

She didn't trust me, but she was right not to. One month would never be enough when I needed her by my side. But the month itself was little more than semantics. It was definitely long enough to get her to agree to remain with me.

I almost laughed at myself. I'd never tolerated humans well—that was understatement—yet here I was, negotiating to keep one.

Baby steps, as humans liked to say. I needed a virgin to secure my reign, but I needed her to come to me willingly.

I withheld a sigh. Oh, to be human, and behave as if I had all the time in the world when in reality, they had so little.

Leia watched me, and a shiver of anticipation worked through my body. Sitting with her so close was the most exquisite torture. Her scent almost drowned me, yet I couldn't prevent myself from taking breath after breath of it. If I hyperventilated, there was no better excuse than the scent of a virgin, especially one who tempted me like this.

The mere thought of having her in my house was almost enough to make me come in my pants...but I had no intention of coming anywhere other than her body. And that would require careful seduction.

I flipped through the paperwork and extracted the final contract Jason had made legal draw up.

"If you could just sign here, Miss Boucher." I indicated the dotted line and reached to my inside pocket for a pen.

She swallowed, the sound audible, transmitting her fear. "You brought an actual contract for this eventuality? You knew I'd agree?"

It had been mostly a certainty—humans always went with the least bad thing. And a month with me paled in comparison to losing every other element of her life. "Hoped."

As she glanced at me, more suspicion in her eyes, I stood and strolled casually to the fireplace, glancing up at the portrait of the woman above. It was her mother, but Leia didn't know I knew that. I'd been involved with this family since they started in Baton Rouge. I'd grieved for each of them as they'd died, even Camille, although we'd lost touch after Father...

I shook my head and stopped the thoughts of the past. There was no point to them now. I had too much future to secure to get lost in memories.

Perhaps my link to Leia's family line had been fate, although no other had ever held the same pull for me as Leia. "Would you like to show me around?"

Her head whipped up, her eyes meeting mine as I asked my question.

"The house won't be yours." Her words were cold. "You don't need to see it."

"I know. Consider me an interested friend." I injected just enough threat into my words that she flinched and shoved the signed contract in my direction before standing and walking to the door.

She didn't even glance over her shoulder before she started talking.

"Pretty self-explanatory. Entrance hall with a main staircase." Then she pointed like she was bored. "Formal dining over there, we were just in the old drawing room. Kitchen at the back and a sitting room. There's a TV in there but—" She broke off and chuckled. "That hasn't worked since they turned off the cable last month."

I turned a slow circle, taking in the crown molding that needed repair, the paint that was chipping off, the floor that was scraped and worn, and the furnishings that were battered and scuffed. None of the furniture was antique or original to the house, and nothing was as I remembered. I opened my mouth to ask about a particular console table I'd always admired, but that would give too much away, so I just murmured consideringly instead.

"What?" Leia asked.

"Nothing." I leaned closer to her, breathing her in. "Just thinking I maybe had a lucky break. This place needs a fuck-ton of money spent on it."

Her glance should have withered me. But it excited me, instead. She had spirit, and that was arousing.

"Not yours to worry about," she said. "Not yours at all now."

Not taking my gaze from hers, I inclined my head, happy to give her this point, to let her win a few battles. I intended to win a lot more before our time together ended.

I intended to claim her. I'd only heard stories of true mates, but the more time I spent with Leia, the surer I was. And a true mate—maybe the first in generations in my line—meant no one would dare challenge me once I'd claimed her.

Something in her blood called to me. I could hear it thrumming through her veins, and it perfumed the air of any room she stood in. It was delectable, and I could almost taste it on my tongue. My fangs ached with need, and my cock thickened.

I'd been in the company of virgins before—long before I'd ever needed one—and they were all young. Mere slips of girls with nothing in their heads. But their blood hadn't called to mine the way Leia's did. She was like a walking enchantment.

"And upstairs?" I glanced at the staircase. It needed attention, too.

Her eyes narrowed familiarly. "That's my *private* space."

"Absolutely." I nudged against her, the touch so brief it could have been accidental, but her heartrate kicked up, signaling her awareness of me. "But your contracted expectation to privacy only applies to *my* home. However, in the spirit of goodwill…" I moved away, putting distance between us, even though I would have been happier to take her with me.

I peered back into the drawing room. Jean was snoring, oblivious to the fact he'd gifted me his daughter, leaving me in the perfect position to stake my claim. "I'll make arrangements for your father to attend rehab."

"As we discussed." Her response was sharp, like I might go back on our agreement, and I almost grinned at her lack of thanks. But her outer confidence belied her obvious anxiety.

Every challenge she offered made me more sure she was meant for me. I'd never felt more alive than right now, standing alongside her in a house that was more hole than *whole*.

And fuck… my *true mate* was a *virgin*. It was like winning the lottery twice. A total mindfuck. A virgin *and* a true mate—not something I'd ever expected to find, even though I'd waited as long as

I could on the off chance that true mates were real and there was one out there for me.

I always would have had to find a virgin to secure my reign after Father. None of us had expected the end when it came, though, and it had left me weaker than I liked. But humans.

Fucking humans.

Still, that part was unavoidable. Non-negotiable. I needed a virgin. Virgins were human. Vampire women were too long-lived. Therefore, that translated to *me* fucking a human.

But my true mate… my true mate could have been vampire. And although no one had forged a true mate bond in generations, a secret part of me had hoped to find mine. In stories, it was a mythical state of being. In reality, my true mate would amplify my vampire powers—I'd be stealthier, faster, stronger, heal quicker, and I'd have increased powers of compulsion.

In return, my mate would benefit from amplification herself. I'd never wanted to give even a part of myself to anyone, but now I longed to. I wanted to forge that bond, to share some of my abilities. Things that would keep her safe, like quicker healing, protection from other vampires, greater strength.

I could have claimed anyone as a simple mate, someone to rule alongside me. But I hadn't wanted to just claim anyone. I didn't have a problem finding women to fuck me, and I hadn't wanted to mate just anyone to be my queen. So I'd held out for the legend, for the promise of power and a rule stronger than my father's. Maybe if I had that, I wouldn't end the same way he had. Or maybe there was a romantic lurking somewhere in my creaky old heart.

I brushed aside that ridiculous notion.

No. It was the power a true mate could bring that I really desired. And in my family, that was the kind of power I needed. Lots of it.

I allowed my gaze to linger over Leia again. She'd need protecting. I wanted her close to my side, but bringing her into my world as an unclaimed virgin laid her open to all sorts of power-hungry vampires who might try to make her theirs. Not least my own family. They wouldn't hesitate to try to usurp my place as the new king.

My fingers formed a fist. It was a tricky line to walk, a tricky balance to keep. But Leia was mine, and she'd be at my side willingly by the end of this month, if it even took that long. Of that, I had no doubt.

When she looked at me, her cheeks red, I glanced away. "Sorry." I wasn't sorry at all. "I shouldn't stare."

She parted her lips but said nothing.

I leaned closer to her, and she watched me, truly prey caught in my gaze. She let out a startled whimper as I bent so close our lips almost touched.

"I think I'm going to enjoy this, Miss Boucher." When I touched my mouth against hers, it was faint and fleeting, and longing sent thin threads through me, tying me into tiny, painful knots as the start of our bond developed.

Before I could tease myself any more, I pulled away. "I'll be back for you later tonight. In the meantime, I'll make all the arrangements we've discussed."

I returned to the drawing room and picked up her signed contract before folding it into three and tucking it into my pocket. Then I reclaimed the rest of Jean Boucher's file.

"You won't be required at The Pour House today," I said as I let myself out into the mid-morning Louisiana sun, fighting against the ache in my gums.

If Leia made a response, it was contained behind the closed door, and it probably wasn't one I'd have wanted to hear anyway. I grinned as I strode down the steps, my attention on the cracked and decaying stone under my feet. Creepers wound around the columns, anchoring themselves to the masonry, and I wouldn't have liked to take my chances leaning against the balcony balustrade.

So much work to undertake to bring this place anywhere near to its former glory.

And my mate planned to do it all herself, it seemed.

I slipped my sunglasses on as I crossed the driveway to where Jenkins was still waiting, and as I slid into the backseat, I already had my phone to my ear.

"Yeah?"

I shook my head. Benedict rarely sounded respectful. "She's coming to live with me. Can you get everything ready?"

There was a moment's pause. "Yes, absolutely."

"And Ben?"

Another pause. "Yeah?" This time the word was hesitant, and I grinned as we traveled back into town, familiar scenery hurtling by and the dry AC in my car keeping the worst of the humidity at bay.

"You're managing a bar for the next month."

Benedict chuckled. "Now that, I can definitely do. So what made you call in the sub-clause?"

"She's everything I need." I'd intended to keep things vague, but I pressed the button to roll the privacy screen into place and filled Benedict in. He needed to know if he was going to help me. "I need to protect her from the others, though. She's mine for a month. That's the only time I have to spend with her and make her want to stay."

Benedict hissed an inhale through his teeth. "But she's a human. What have you found?"

I chuckled. "What haven't I found? A virgin to cement my ascension to the throne. More. But Sebastian could present a...problem."

My mind whirled as I spoke. Sebastian was my younger brother. He'd always been the spare to my heir, and he'd always been jealous. He'd see Leia as his opportunity to step into my place. Most likely by killing her to prevent my claim on a virgin. He was a ruthless son of a bitch, and he knew I'd never be officially recognized as king without staking my claim to a virgin to heighten my powers.

Benedict sighed. "You never take the easy route, Nic. When do you need me at the bar?"

"As soon as possible. I told Leia she's not needed there today. I'll collect her later. I want to talk to my staff before I bring her home." My chef would probably be most pleased of all—finally, someone to cook for.

"You got Jason on security detail?" Of course, Benedict was still focused on practicalities.

"Yes. And I'll warn him about Seb." I blew out a sigh. If only vampire families weren't so bloodthirsty.

"Maybe he won't try anything." Benedict's hopeful tone made me chuckle.

"Mm... History doesn't permit me that degree of optimism."

Benedict chuckled too. "Okay, I'll grab the address of this bar I'm managing from our files, and I'll head straight there after I make any other necessary arrangements for her stay."

"I think the bar's going to need some work." If it was anything like the house, it would need a complete overhaul. I was confident Benedict could handle it, though.

We finished the call, and I grinned as I slipped my phone away and considered all of the changes I needed to make my home a place where Leia would want to spend time. My seduction of her would start today.

My plantation home was everything hers should have been…*could* have been. Fucking *would have been* if her father hadn't spent all the family money on drink and gambling. If he'd been fucking man enough to earn some himself.

A sliver of guilt sliced through me at how many days I'd allowed him to prop up at a poker or blackjack table at La Petite Mort. But I pushed it away. I ran a business. The people who gave me their money were of no concern to me—especially when they were willing to part with such valuable things as Jean Boucher apparently was.

Almost made me want to believe in fate.

"We've arrived at La Petite Mort, sir." Jenkins's voice was tinny, his announcement unnecessary as it crackled through the car's audio system.

"It won't be a late night today, Jenkins. We'll be collecting Leia Boucher to take her to my home with me." I opened the door and got out before he replied, my head already occupied with thoughts of Leia and the way her scent wove right through me, drumming up a thirst like I'd never known.

As soon as I entered my office, I cleared my schedule for the rest of the afternoon and spent my time on the phone to my housekeeper. "Prepare the east wing, please Mrs. Ames, I'm expecting a guest."

"Wonderful, Mr. Dupont." There was a smile in her voice as she spoke. "Do I know the..." She paused. "Gentleman?"

I grinned at her clumsy attempt to get the information she wanted.

"Her name is Leia Boucher, and she's to have anything she wants while she's with us. Food, entertainment, the ability to roam at her will." I paused and rethought. "But of course, no access to my private quarters."

"Of course, Mr. Dupont. And this really is wonderful news. I'll see to the preparations myself, and I'm sure Chef will want to come up with an entirely new menu." She already sounded flustered, but she'd worked for me for a long time, and I knew she had everything in hand.

"Excellent. She'll arrive home with me this evening." Sudden excitement zinged through me at seeing Leia again, *smelling* Leia again, but I tamped it down. I needed her to ensure I'd cement my true place, and I couldn't allow *anything* to interfere with that—especially not the sloppiness of emotion. Plus she was human, and no human was worth this degree of excitement, in my experience.

This situation required the ultimate control. But I wasn't like my siblings. I could control myself, and had for years. I used donor bags of blood for feeding so I'd never lose myself to blood lust—no one could ever lust after the disgusting taste of this blood—and I could absolutely claim a virgin for her power without giving in to the baser mating instincts of my kind. It could perhaps be the ultimate business arrangement.

My entire life was a lesson in control—tempting others to lose theirs while honing my own.

All I had to do with Leia was make her comfortable enough to accept me… To *offer* herself to me within one month, and my entire future was secured.

Yes, that was all.

But the words *true mate* lingered in my thoughts before I had a chance to dismiss them.

Chapter 5 - Leia

If Nicolas Dupont thought I was just gonna stay home and wait around for him like some weird prom date pick-up, he could think again. That was absolute crap. No guy told me what to do. No guy had even tried since I started running The Pour House. Well, maybe some had tried, but I'd ignored them all.

Like I was ignoring Dupont now as I sorted some of the files in the office behind the kitchen at the bar and changed the combination on the safe out of sheer habit—however much that action was a day late and way the hell more than a dollar short.

But I was used to being my own boss, and just handing the business over to someone else for a month wasn't something I was happy to do. I wanted to meet this guy Dupont was installing, make sure he knew how to run things, that he got on with my regulars. I really didn't want to come back to no business because it had been left in the hands of someone who had no clue how to run a bar.

I'd brought Dad with me, too—I didn't trust him enough to leave him at home by himself. He probably couldn't do anything, but the man seemed to open lines of credit for himself as easy as breathing, so it was better not to take chances. He was up front propped between Harry and Pierre, and they were probably sick of babysitting duty already.

I slammed the top drawer closed—that one had been sticky as long as I could remember—and walked through the kitchen then stopped as I caught sight of a man I'd never met making himself at home behind my bar.

From the back, he reminded me of Nicolas Dupont—he was tall and his shoulders were broad, and something about the strength in his muscles made me think of the other man—but when he turned in my direction, there was nothing secretive or stormy about his almost aqua eyes, and his ready smile was a welcome change to the more predatory one Dupont seemed to favor.

I shuddered just thinking about Dupont's smile…his mouth. Except it wasn't really a shudder; it was more of a shiver of anticipation—and an unwelcome one, too. Damn horny, traitorous body.

Well, I'd make my way back here as soon as I could. The more I pondered my situation, the more I considered the contract, the more I decided there was probably a loophole. All contracts had them. I just had to find this one. That would put a stop to my body wanting to do its own thing.

I just had to bide my time while I figured my way out.

"Can I help you?" I approached the stranger—I had a fair idea why this guy was here, but I folded my arms as I looked him over. "Customers don't usually make their own drinks at my bar."

His smile widened as he stepped forward. "What? You don't believe in the honor system?" His lips formed a small pout as I slowly shook my head. Then he was back to grinning. "I believe you were expecting me? I'm Benedict Rousseau, temporary bar manager at your service."

He swept a small bow, and I bit back an unexpected chuckle. Without missing a beat, he turned and served a customer, even recommending the beer he thought the guy should try.

I nodded at the customer's back as he walked away. "You done this kind of thing before, Benedict?" I didn't want to sound too friendly or welcoming. I was doing all this shit under protest. I literally didn't have a choice.

"I guess you could say that." He nodded. "I've amassed a lot of experience in a lot of different areas over the years, and bar keeping is just one of my many talents."

"Jeez. With yourself around, you certainly don't need a fan club," I muttered, then blushed when he seemed to pick up my quiet words and laughed.

"Some free advice for you," he replied. "Be your own biggest fan."

I rolled my eyes. "Yeah. Thanks."

"All the best bartenders give advice." He glanced at where Pierre and Harry still had Dad between them. "They look like good guys."

"Yeah, they're great." I started to relax. They'd keep Benedict under control for me. "Regulars, too. Come and meet them."

Benedict put a glass he'd been wiping back in the rack above the bar and followed me toward Harry and Pierre's booth. It had gotten to the stage where I could've just labelled it; no one else ever sat there.

"Hey, cher." Harry's eyes crinkled around the corners as he smiled, and I grinned back.

"Hi, Harry, just wanted to introduce you to Benedict. He'll be managing the bar while I…"

"She's going on vacation," Dad interjected, and Benedict frowned slightly, just a quick tug at the center of his eyebrows before his expression smoothed out again. Probably so fleeting that no one else even saw it.

Pierre cocked his head, his gaze quizzical. "Vacation?" He and his brother knew enough about my business to be aware that I couldn't possibly afford time away, never mind an actual trip somewhere.

"Mysterious benefactor. She's a lucky girl, my Leia." Dad grinned broadly like he had something to be proud of, and this time Harry did frown.

I stopped looking at him and focused on Pierre instead. I didn't want to talk to Dad. He'd gambled me away, and now he seemed pleased with himself over it. "I'll be gone for a month, so Benedict will be managing The Pour House while I'm away."

Pierre nodded. "Sounds like a good plan." He cast some side-eye toward Dad.

"Well, anything you need, Benedict." Harry half-rose and extended his hand to Benedict. "Anyone helping Leia out earns our help in return."

Benedict nodded as he clasped Harry's palm. "Just Ben is fine, and thank you. I'll be sure to let you know if I think of anything." Then he nodded toward Dad. "You'll be collected tomorrow to start your own vacation."

"*My* vacation?" Dad's eyes widened. "That's not something I agreed to."

"Perhaps not." Benedict flattened his lips and the corners of his mouth dipped. "But Nic was pretty insistent. You've been booked for a month's rehabilitation therapy, and you'll be assessed again at the end of the month."

Nic. I couldn't imagine referring to Nicolas Dupont so informally, but the idea teased a thrill of excitement through me. I quickly squashed it, though. I needed to get through this month without memories of the man's lips and tongue.

And his hands. Fuck, his hands as they'd moved heat over my skin. I'd wanted him to touch me again. Anywhere. Everywhere. But that wasn't going to help me.

"You'd look churlish and ungrateful to refuse help, Jean," Harry cautioned, his expression stony as he watched Dad glare at no one in particular.

Benedict shrugged, but the movement was tight. "I guess change is hard. I'd advise that turning up there with a hangover might not look great, though."

"We've got him, and we'll make sure he doesn't lose himself in a bottle tonight," Pierre said. Then he looked at me. "You go and enjoy your time. Don't worry about a thing."

I nodded, gratitude warming me that these men cared enough to help. Maybe not Benedict—I didn't know him—but I couldn't have gotten this far without Harry and Pierre at my back, watching over me.

Benedict turned to me. "I think you should go home and pack." The gentleness in his eyes made it more of a suggestion and less of an instruction, but it was still a statement that didn't have *no* as an answer.

"That won't take long." I answered with a hair flip and an annoying nervous giggle that slipped out without my permission. I didn't have a great deal worth taking anywhere, especially given I didn't entirely know what was expected of me. Anxiety prickled up my cheeks. If Dupont expected ballgowns and evening dresses, he'd called in the wrong contract.

"Good luck." Dad raised his glass in my direction, his eyes gleaming a little too brightly.

"Cut him off now," I said quietly, and Benedict and Harry nodded.

"We'll make sure he gets to where he needs to be," Harry said, and I nodded before turning to the door.

Every step across the bar was one I had to think about. There were nights when I hadn't wanted to leave because it meant returning home to another place that hemorrhaged money faster than I could earn it. But today I didn't want to leave because I was scared of the unknown and what I would find there.

And when I closed my eyes, the looming figure I saw was most definitely Nicolas Dupont.

***

The black limo sat purring in my driveway. I'd been ignoring it for fifteen minutes already, unable to make myself leave my home. I wanted to hang onto the furniture, the drapes, the doorframes so no one could remove me.

But in reality, I looked in a mirror spotty with dust and age blemishes, patted my hair, smoothed the lip gloss I was unaccustomed to wearing from the edges of my lips, and straightened my spine.

I could do this. I could walk across my cracked and overgrown driveway and be driven somewhere I didn't know with a stranger I'd only met once.

Twice, my traitorous mind supplied, but at least one of those meetings didn't include a handshake or names, so it didn't count.

A driver, complete with cap, sunglasses and leather driving gloves, climbed out of the front and walked around to open the back door for me.

I glanced in the limo before I slid onto the seat. "No Mr. Dupont?"

My stomach did that weird thing between relief and disappointment. *Nausea*, that was probably better known as.

"Mr. Dupont sends his regrets, but he's been delayed at La Petite Mort."

My throat dried at the mention of Dupont's casino, but I swallowed and sat inside the car.

"He said for you to make yourself comfortable and help yourself to a drink." The driver waved at a mini-bar.

"Thank you—" I paused. "I'm sorry, I don't know your name."

"Jenkins, Miss Boucher."

"Thank you, Mr. Jenkins," I said, and one corner of his mouth tipped up.

"My pleasure."

As the car pulled away from my house, I stared at my hands. I didn't need to look at my home. It wouldn't be the last time I saw it. It wasn't like I needed to commit it to memory or anything.

My fingers twisted together and my skin paled. "Where exactly are we going?" My voice was steady and calm, but even in his sunglasses, I got the sense Jenkins was watching me in the rearview mirror as he answered.

"Mr. Dupont lives a little farther out on the south side of the city."

I nodded like I'd known that much while I tried to imagine what his house might look like.

Traffic was light for our journey, and we looped around the city rather than driving through, giving me a view of spread-out homes, mailboxes with no house in sight along the rutted tire tracks that led away between fields, and barely moving bayous with tree trunks rooted in them.

As those views gave way to something greener, and swamp gave way to grass, live oak trees took over, the Spanish moss growing with far more decorum and grace than it ever grew by my property, hanging in delicate fronds.

The car slowed and Mr. Jenkins made a wide turn onto a sweeping driveway that led to a large white home. I sat forward, almost on the edge of my seat as I watched it grow bigger as we approached.

"Beautiful," I whispered.

"Isn't it?" Mr. Jenkins half-turned toward me. "It's been in Mr. Dupont's family for centuries."

It was larger than my house, with a sweeping balcony across the front, columns that soared higher than I could dream of, and a large dome on top. Its majesty was everything my house deserved, and my gut twisted again as I thought of Dad's actions that had resulted in the current state of our home.

The outside of Dupont's house gleamed as if freshly painted or cleaned, and the driveway looked as if it didn't dare crack or sink.

God alone knew what I was going to have to do for one month to have a hope of reinstating my house to even half of this glory.

When the car stopped at the bottom of the wide steps, I sat for a moment, not even moving to unbuckle my seatbelt. I'd expected a grand lifestyle from Dupont, but I glanced at my jeans and well-worn shirt and cringed a little. This wasn't my world. Not even close.

I battled every day for what I had, I clawed my way to it, and I wasn't ashamed of it, but I knew where I belonged, and it wasn't with Nicolas Dupont, and it wasn't here.

Mr. Jenkins opened the door, and before I'd even climbed out, a butler stood at the top of the stairs, his hands at his sides as he waited for me to join him. Alongside him stood an older lady in a navy-blue skirt and jacket over a white blouse.

The butler bowed slightly as I arrived next to him.

"Miss Boucher," he murmured. "Welcome to *Vitam Immortalem.*"

"Thank you." Between the name of his casino and the name of his house, Dupont certainly had an odd sense of humor.

I stepped inside the house and the butler closed the heat out, cocooning us in a space as quiet as the grave. For a moment I didn't even breathe.

"Are you all right, my dear? You needn't worry. The wards here are very old and will protect you." The butler touched my arm, and normal household noises seemed to come rushing back as my mind unmuffled. "Would you like me to show you around a little?"

I narrowed my eyes slightly at the obvious eccentricities of the man. *Wards*? "Thank you,

Mr.....?" I didn't look at him as I spoke. There was too much to take in.

A wide staircase that started to my right curved up to the second floor, but more steps just beyond that led downward. A beautiful hardwood floor swept forward, appearing to cover acres of ground, before passing seamlessly through an archway supported by more beautiful Grecian-style columns. A grand piano sat further inside the room, as well as gleaming wood sideboards and a couple of oversized Asian vases that could have originated with the Ming Dynasty for all I knew.

The butler laughed and gestured to the lady with him. "I'm Baldwin, and this is Mrs. Ames."

"Thank you, Mr. Baldwin."

"I'll just show you the basics. Chef is very excited you're here and is preparing quite the feast. It's not often we have guests."

I nodded again, like I'd morphed into some sort of bobble-headed toy. There was no way I'd own a place like this and not have guests for most of the year. It was how I imagined every boutique hotel I couldn't afford to visit—exquisite.

"If I owned this place, I might pay people to visit me just so I could show it off." I didn't mean to speak out loud, but Mr. Baldwin laughed.

"Then maybe I shouldn't boast of the amenities?" He gestured toward the staircase that disappeared below the house. "In the basement, you'll find a home cinema, a swimming pool, and the gym. But if you follow me up the staircase, I'll show you to the east wing, where you have your own suite of rooms."

I chuckled. "Is the west wing reserved for the president?"

Mr. Baldwin paused for a moment, his feet still on the stairs before he regained his forward momentum.

"The west wing is the master's personal quarters. They're strictly off limits to everybody, and the one place you really can't go." He turned to me at the top of the staircase, his jaw firm, his eyes serious. Then he smiled. "But the rest of the house is yours to explore and enjoy. This way, please."

He led me between wide double doors into a tastefully decorated hallway, where everything was soft and a shade of cream, but I cast a glance over my shoulder at matching double doors that were firmly closed.

The area I wasn't allowed. That was interesting… and possibly a reason I could use to terminate our contract early if it had something to do with whatever Dupont was obviously holding back from me about our deal. The loophole I was looking for. Maybe Dupont was involved in criminal activity and needed me with him so he'd look respectable? But surely not…

I chewed my lip. Well, it wouldn't be the first time a business was used as a front for something else, and if I could find out what, I could get away.

So I had to know.

I returned my attention to Mr. Baldwin as he opened a door and strode into a room that could have belonged to royalty. There was a large four-poster bed on a small raised platform, and I tore my gaze away before an unexpected visual of Nicolas Dupont, his body over mine and the sheets rumpled around us, solidified in my mind.

"There's a small seating area." Mr. Baldwin spoke unnecessarily as he pointed beyond the bed. "And through this door, your bathroom."

I peered into the biggest bathroom I'd ever seen, and it was a beautiful mix between old-world style and shower controls that looked space-age. "Wow."

Mr. Baldwin smiled, his eyes lighting with what looked like pride. "And the other door is your walk-in closet." He led me into a room bigger than the square footage of The Pour House and I gasped.

There were already gowns hanging on some of the rails, and I reached out to touch one before retracting my hand.

"If there's anything you don't like, I can arrange to have it sent away, but the master felt sure these would be to your liking."

I pressed my lips together to prevent myself from agreeing, holy crap, *yes*, I liked them very much. But I didn't stop my head from nodding, and the movement gave me away.

Mr. Baldwin laughed again and clapped his hands. "Very good. But we'll have to cut the tour short here or Chef will send out a search party. If you'd like to follow me to the dining room?" It wasn't simply a polite request, so I fell in line behind him, my stomach churning with anxiety as we walked back across the room.

And I still couldn't look at the bed.

Mr. Baldwin hurried back down the stairs, suddenly taking on a tour guide persona as he flung his arms out to the left and right. "This is the formal drawing room. The sitting room. Study. Library."

Wait…what? I slowed my steps then backtracked to the room he'd pointed into last. Floor to ceiling bookshelves dominated the space, and there were ladders hooked over rails at various points around the room. I stepped inside, already inhaling the smell of leather and pages and ink.

"My dear?" Mr. Baldwin's voice floated back down the hallway, and I peered around the doorway toward him.

"Sorry. I… I like this room."

"A very good choice." He hurried toward me, his shoes striking the wooden floor with each step. "It's one of my favorite rooms, too." He sighed. "Alas, we don't have time to discuss the books now. Chef has a lot of knives in his kitchen." He broke off and chuckled. Then he started to walk and point again. "Formal dining room. Family dining room, and the kitchen is through that door there. I'm sure the master would let you in there, but maybe while Chef's not around." He winked. "Where would you like to eat tonight?"

I glanced around. "Is it… Is it just me?"

I glanced around like I almost expected Nicolas Dupont to appear through the walls or hurtle through a window. I hated feeling so insecure, but this house wasn't my natural environment, and I didn't feel safe here.

Well, no. That wasn't quite it. It wasn't safety so much as I didn't trust my surroundings.

Fuck it. I didn't trust *myself.*

A masculine, spicy scent lingered in the air in nearly every room, and I knew exactly who it belonged to.

"For now." Mr. Baldwin nodded. "The master has been further delayed at——"

"At the casino." I jumped in and finished his sentence, and he nodded.

Disappointment niggled at me, but I pushed it away and waited for the relief I should feel instead. I needed to be relieved that I was here alone.

Perhaps my whole month would fly by like this. Just me and that fantastic library. Alone. In Dupont's house.

Now that was the kind of vacation I could get behind.

"I guess I could go family dining room? I'm not sure I'm dressed for formal." And I definitely didn't need to be at the end of the huge banquet table I'd glimpsed through the doorway.

"Perfect." He led me in and set a place at the table before stopping on his way to the door. "Chef will be in with your meal in a moment."

I unfolded my napkin and set it over my lap, and when I looked up, Mr. Baldwin had left the room.

I glanced around, taking in the sumptuous designs and textures in the decoration and finishes of the room. I was sitting at a table that looked like an antique. In the fucking *least* formal of the dining rooms. I was more used to making do with badly put together furniture I'd assembled from Ikea knockoffs. A knock at the door startled me, and a man stepped in, a huge try of food in his arms.

"Good evening," he said, and I half-stood to return his greeting.

My napkin slid from my lap, and I bent to retrieve it but ended up sitting back in my chair with no grace at all.

"Fresh from the kitchen." A woman rushed in behind the man, a tray stand clutched in one of her hands. "I'm Emma. I work for Mr. Dupont, and this is Chef."

"Just… Chef?" I lifted an eyebrow.

"I am what I do," he confirmed as he set up the tray and started unloading plates in front of me.

I watched pasta dishes and a hamburger and risotto and a surf and turf platter hit the table, and I blew out a breath. "Are we expecting more guests or…or someone else?"

Maybe Nicolas Dupont wasn't held up at work anymore. My anxiety roared back to life, and I drummed my fingertips on the gleaming wood.

"I got a little carried away, perhaps." Chef ran his gaze over the food.

"Or maybe not carried away enough?" Emma suggested. "Maybe she prefers something else?"

"Oh, no! I... There's no way I can eat so much food. Will you join me?" I gestured to the chairs opposite me.

Emma darted a quick glance at Chef. "Uh, we're staff. We're not allowed to eat while on duty."

"Oh, shit. Sorry." I cringed. "Sorry again. I mean, I don't want to get you in trouble with Mr. Dupont." I scooped some pasta onto my plate. "I'll just have a little of everything."

Chef watched me carefully while I ate, nodding his approval every time I murmured appreciation for his food, and Emma chatted, telling me a little about the various antiques in the room and details about the house and grounds. When I finally pushed my plate away, Chef looked at Emma, triumph shining in his eyes.

"See! I told you I've still got it."

I laughed. "I don't know what you think you lost, but it's certainly not the ability to cook." I tried to stifle a yawn but ended up hiding my face behind my hands as it took control. "I'm sorry. I have no idea why I'm so tired."

Dusk had fallen outside, but it was nowhere near late. Something about being at Dupont's house seemed to have let my body know I no longer needed to stay up until hella late o'clock working, and exhaustion raced through my veins, relaxing my muscles and fogging my thoughts.

"Would you like me to show you to your room?" Emma paused in her removal of the plates from the table.

I smiled at her. "No, thank you. Mr. Baldwin already showed me. West wing, right?"

"East." She made the correction sharply and fast. "I mean, the west wing is off limits."

"Shoot. Yeah. Sorry. I meant east." I tapped my forehead. "I'm just tired."

I gazed at the closed west wing doors as I climbed the stairs. If it wasn't a criminal mastermind headquarters, I had no idea what could be behind there that Dupont was so protective of, but I hadn't been lying about being tired. Knowing what Dupont kept in the rooms I wasn't allowed in would keep until at least tomorrow.

But those rooms were likely my key to leaving.

As I walked toward my room, the shadows moved, and I sucked in a harsh breath.

Nicolas Dupont's low chuckle brushed over my skin as he stepped away from the wall. "I didn't mean to startle you."

"Oh!" The sound flew from my mouth. I hadn't expected… I narrowed my eyes a little. What was he doing here? Waiting to make a move? I straightened my shoulders, trying to project confidence. "You didn't startle me."

Dupont remained quiet, his left hand forming a loose fist at his side as he watched me. His pupils dilated as an unexpected rush of desire flooded me, and his chest heaved as he breathed in.

I backed up a little, and my ass grazed the door behind me. "We had a deal, remember. I'm here to settle a debt. I said no sex."

He hummed, the sound a mild disagreement. "Nope. You said no *sleeping with me*. I can almost guarantee there'd be no sleeping involved if you were to spend the night in my bed." He stepped closer and took a lock of my hair between his finger and thumb, watching the strands as he rubbed them gently. "And I can definitely guarantee your satisfaction."

He met my eyes, and his seemed to swirl with a beautiful oncoming storm.

"No." I jerked back. "I've told you I don't want you, and for you to continue after I've told you that would be rape."

His eyes flashed then. The storm had arrived, and I'd been wrong about beauty. It was a wicked, wicked storm.

"Rape?" His voice was a low growl. "I would never *rape*." He stepped away from me, putting the illusion of distance between us before leaning almost close enough that his lips grazed my ear. "When we have sex, Miss Boucher—which is definitely a *when*, not an *if*—it will be because you're begging me for what you want."

Then he pivoted and strode away down the hall, leaving his now familiar scent and confusion swirling around me as my body and mind warred about what they wanted.

I glared at his retreating back, watching him the whole way down the corridor, my gaze so heavy he should have combusted under the weight and anger I tried to channel. Even when he was out of sight, he still remained in my head.

That fucking guy.

Chapter 6 - Nic

My fangs descended as I walked away, and I couldn't glance back, although the weight of Leia's gaze was heavy on my back. I knew what I'd see. She wanted me, but she also felt that she needed to reject me. But if I saw too much of her desire, maybe I wouldn't be strong enough to walk away.

And I meant what I'd told her. I wanted her to beg. Fuck, I wanted her to *beg*. My dick jerked with awareness as I inhaled a lungful of her scent, still so potent even as the distance grew between us. Goddammit. She was all over my house already.

I threw the doors to my private wing open then secured them behind me, trying to find relief in isolation. Perhaps I just needed to feed and to bathe. Relax.

I heated a bag of blood, although Leia's heartbeat was like a pulse inside me, even with her half the house away. My awareness of her would drive me crazy. And I didn't even fucking drink from humans. Control in *all* things, that was what drove me through all of these decades. Control and power.

But I'd never wanted anything more than I wanted to claim Leia. I wanted to pierce her fragile skin with my fangs and draw on her, filling my mouth with blood that smelled like honey.

My cock hardened but I ignored it and stepped into my bath, groaning as I submerged my body below the water. My muscles were so tight. I wanted Leia's touch on me to relax them. I wanted Leia's touch fucking everywhere.

I wanted her touch, her surrender, her soft noises of desire. I wanted her body to clench around mine.

But I shook my head. I needed her virginity more.

Fucking humans.

I sent a wave of water over the side of the bath as I moved my arm so I could scrub my palms over my face. None of this was helping me relax. I dried off with angry strokes and strode to my bed, my hard cock bouncing against my abs. Needy fucker.

Images of Leia pounded through my head, and as I settled into bed, my hand drifted down my body. With a groan, I took hold of my cock, wrapping my fingers around the shaft, and for a moment, I waited, teasing myself by staying still. My cock pulsed in my hand, thickening as I imagined Leia's touch in place of mine, her gaze on my body.

I jerked upward, pressing harder into my grip at the memory of her parted lips and the touch of her tongue against mine that first night, and I released a harsh exhale as heat raced through my body before coming to rest at the base of my cock.

A bead of precum slid from the tip, and I smeared it over my skin with the pad of my thumb, gritting my teeth to keep my soft hiss inside my throat when I wanted to bellow my need, when I wanted to run to Leia's room and bury myself inside her to ease the desire that burned through me.

Even here, in my space, her scent clung to me, spiking my heartrate as my hand moved to the rhythm of each beat, pushing increasingly harsh breaths from me as I relieved my arousal with firm, efficient strokes. Control in all things.

Tonight wasn't a time for teasing. I just needed Leia out of my system, and I chased her away with each movement even while I invited her closer with every fantasy of her body pressed to mine, her thighs parted in welcome.

I alone would take her virginity, claiming her wholly as mine, never to belong to anyone else.

Power at those thoughts surged through me and my balls tightened, drawing against me before my cock erupted, splattering hot stickiness over my hand and abs. I fought to control my breaths and closed my eyes against a sudden memory of Leia's tongue. I could almost feel it moving over my skin, tasting me, and I groaned as my dick jerked again, fresh arousal already evident.

Maybe my virgin would be the death of me yet.

***

I slept badly, my skin still on fire, my dick uncomfortably hard all night. When I woke before the sun, I lay on my back, one arm flung over my eyes as I fought against the urge to relieve myself again.

Leia needed to come to me willingly. I couldn't take her by force or cajole her, but perhaps I could welcome her, provide the finer things in life—the things she undoubtedly deserved but had never been given or taken for herself before.

Nothing would be too much or beyond my reach. More gowns like those I'd already provided, jewels to adorn her and shimmer against her skin. Food such as she'd never sampled before—although Chef had already begun the culinary assault, teasing her tastebuds with a wide array of dishes.

It was up to me to awaken her other hungers, make her realize all the opportunities that could be hers if she just chose to be mine. And that could start today. By the time dawn had brightened the sky, I'd made several calls to staff at the casino and even within the house, and everyone was standing by to carry out my instructions.

I lingered outside the open double doors to the east wing, ridiculous and unfamiliar uncertainty shredding my nerves. The first stirrings of the human female inside reached my ears, and my awareness of her sent my pulse rocketing again. But I clamped down on my fierce arousal. I could control myself.

I could control this seduction. *I* was seducing *her*. Not the other way around.

When she appeared from her rooms in a swirl of floral scent and bright-eyed readiness for a new day, she paused as she caught sight of me.

I skimmed my gaze over her, approval flaring inside me at her choice of clothing from the closet

I'd stocked. The jeans fit her as I'd expected, and the T-shirt clung in all the right places. I glanced away, deliberately disinterested, even as I regulated my words and tone. "Is that what you're planning to wear?"

Defiance flashed in her eyes as she tensed her jaw, the movement drawing my gaze to the pulse that beat in her neck, and I curled my hands into tight fists like that alone would prevent me walking to her and kissing my way from her ear to her collarbone.

"For just hanging around your library? I think so." She started to walk past me, but I stopped her with my hand on her forearm, and we both inhaled sharply at the unexpected contact.

I hadn't intended to touch her, and I drew way, clasping my hands behind my back as I spoke. "Chef has prepared a meal to break your fast, and then you'll accompany me to La Petite Mort."

She shivered briefly and cut her gaze quickly to me then away again. "I don't think accompanying you *there*—" she spat the word "—was part of our deal."

I grinned. Negotiations, using words and desires to pin people where I wanted them, was part of my business. This was a familiar area to me, and I loved it.

"Ahh, but Miss Boucher," I said, the words sleek and soft as they left my mouth. "This is the very *essence* of my deal. I believe I told you I am in need of *a companion to accompany me to some forthcoming events with my family and my business associates.* You preferred the term *arm candy.*"

I allowed my lip to curl derisively for a moment, but her eyes widened, and I could see the exact moment she recalled our initial conversation.

But then Leia straightened her shoulders. "Well, if it's only the casino, this outfit's okay."

I shrugged. As long as she didn't parade there nude, I really had no preference to what she wore, and I was used to the dance of giving away small wins for inconsequential battles while I kept my sights on the outcome of the war.

"As you wish. Now, Chef will wonder where you are." I turned and led her down the stairs, aware the whole way of her gaze, it's heat laser-like as she aimed it at the back of my head.

I led her to the family dining room, where the table almost groaned under breakfast food. Chef had arranged fresh baked rolls—still steaming— alongside honey-butter, cheese grits, buttermilk pancakes, scrambled eggs, sausage links, crispy fried bacon and delicate beignets alongside a coffee pot and a pitcher of fresh orange juice.

Baldwin observed us from a corner, and as he offered me a small bow, I nodded my acknowledgement.

"Who else is coming for breakfast?" Leia whirled to face me as she spoke.

"No one." I almost laughed at the idea I might invite humans into my home to sit around a table and eat. I didn't invite them here for any reason.

Well.

Until now.

One human, and she was decidedly *my* human.

"Miss Boucher, if I may explain?" Baldwin spoke, and Leia glanced at him, her face immediately softening.

My muscles tensed. Something about my butler had acquired my human's trust. Unexpected jealousy at the way Leia relaxed with him burst through my chest, but I tightened my control over my movements as I lowered myself into a chair to watch their exchange.

Baldwin immediately hurried forward and drew out a chair for Leia at the only place setting. "Chef wanted you to try a variety of dishes so you might request your preferences going forward."

Leia nodded. "But there will be so much waste."

I shrugged a lazy shoulder. "I can afford it."

But her gaze cooled as her eyes met mine. That had clearly been the wrong thing to say.

"To ensure your comfort in my home," I finished. I wanted to impress her with all I could provide, not anger her.

"Just sample the things that tempt you, and I can let Chef know what you wish to eat tomorrow," Baldwin said as he reached for the coffee pot and splashed the brown liquid into her mug.

Lea immediately closed her eyes and inhaled deeply. "Gallons of coffee. That's the first thing I'll want." Then she smiled, but her expression soon soured as she looked at me again. She gestured at the food. "What do you recommend?"

I shrugged once more. "All of it will be to Chef's impeccable standard."

"Aren't you eating?" Her question was almost an accusation, but I shook my head.

"I ate earlier. My hunger has been…satisfied." *Lie.* But there were various types of hunger.

Leia blew out a sigh then proceeded to try a little from each plate, and I watched her lips the whole time, imagining them against mine, on my skin, wrapped around my cock. The moan she made when she bit into a beignet sent a direct charge to my cock, and I shifted to rearrange the sudden tent in my pants.

"She'll have the beignets tomorrow," I murmured to Baldwin, and I'd be there to watch every mouthful and the way her tongue caught the remnants of powdered sugar from her lips.

Leia glared at me but didn't disagree.

"Are you sated? Or do you desire anything further?" I watched her closely as I asked the question, and her pupils dilated as she looked at me, but she shook her head.

Then she stood and left her napkin neatly by her plate. "No, let's get this *take your hostage to work day* over with."

"Miss Boucher." My words offered no hint that she needed to employ caution in her words. Only amusement at what she'd said. "Please. You're not my hostage. You're my sub-clause."

She glared at me again but looked away as her lips twitched.

***

I threw open the door to La Petite Mort, ready to impress Leia with this part of my empire. I controlled this world. These people were in *my* house and the house always won. Leia was a guest of my home, and I intended to win there, too.

Valérie, my assistant, stepped forward. "Nicolas," she greeted me as she pressed a kiss to each of my cheeks.

I raised an eyebrow as I stepped away. That was a more effusive greeting than usual.

"Miss Boucher, this is my assistant, Valérie. If you need anything at all during your time here, just let her know." I gestured to Valérie as I smiled at Leia. For some reason, I wanted her to know that Valérie and I only had a professional relationship.

"I can sit you in the same seat your father favors, if you like?" Valérie offered an eyebrow raised in challenge, and Leia gasped. "Other than that, I'm pretty busy."

"Valérie." I'd never had to pitch my voice this low to warn her of anything.

She flipped her hair in response and half-turned away from Leia as she faced me. "I have too much to do today to meet the needs of your pet human."

"*Valérie.*" This time I cracked out her name like I'd fired a bullet, and it echoed from the ceiling and walls. "You will show respect to me in my own business, and you will show respect to whomever I choose to bring in as a personal guest. It is not your job to second-guess my decisions, question my motivations, or to cast aspersions on those I choose to spend my time with. Do you understand?"

As two bright red spots appeared in the center of Valérie's cheeks, she inhaled deeply, and her mouth formed a cruel smile.

"Oh, I think I understand perfectly now, Nic." She leaned closer to me, her palm resting on the front of my suit jacket. "She smells divine."

I jerked back, away from her uninvited touch. "Get out of my sight." I ground out each word. Then I turned to Leia. "I have some work to do, but first may I show you around?"

Leia's lip curled like she might refuse with one of the cutting remarks I was becoming used to, but then she darted a glance at Valérie and paled before nodding and taking the arm I offered. It wasn't exactly coming to me willingly—her fear of my assistant was clearly stronger than her desire not to associate with me—but I'd take it.

What I wouldn't accept, however, was Valérie's disrespect, and from the way her glare looked like it might singe Leia, her attitude could very definitely become a problem. One I would have to keep an eye on.

I showed Leia around, then she sat in my office while I completed some paperwork. Something about her presence soothed me, and I snuck looks at her when she was busy observing the casino floor from a large one-way mirror like the one in the meeting room. I wanted to be able to see the humans trying their luck from wherever I was working in the building.

"I can't believe you just used to let my Dad sit down there and give you all his money."

I shrugged and opened my mouth to reply, but her next whispered words stopped me.

"All *my* money."

That much was true, and her raw pain drew a thread of guilt through me. The first ounce of guilt I'd felt in a very long time. Usually, I felt little but contempt for those who threw more and more money into my bank account. I could smell their desperation on it. My fortune stemmed from the deadly sins of humans, and it amused me that they didn't have more discipline.

But it hadn't been Leia down there, spending her money. I couldn't make her father's past mistakes better for Leia, and the fact I had her money tainted my account books.

"I won't take any more," I murmured as I shuffled my papers, trying to look distracted, like her sorrowful words and desperate tone hadn't affected me.

She was silent so long that I glanced up, meeting her gaze as she watched me.

"I mean it. He won't be welcome here." Vehemence underscored my words, and I shocked myself that I'd finally found one human I wouldn't take money from.

All because I'd found one human I was starting to tolerate.

She nodded. "I appreciate that."

If she didn't stop looking at me, her eyes full of gratitude and tenderness, I'd press her to the window and claim her as mine as she watched the people gamble below us. My cock jerked at the thought of her soft skin against mine.

I cleared my throat and stood. "I've arranged for us to have a private lunch on the rooftop terrace."

A lopsided grin graced Leia's lips. "Are you actually going to eat this time?"

I stepped a little closer to her, my shoulder brushing hers as I leaned to open the door. "Oh, I assure you, I'm *very* hungry right now."

Her eyes flared as they met mine, but she averted her gaze and hurried past me into the corridor. Once on the roof, a table with booth seats awaited us under the freestanding awning, and ceiling fans kept us cool in the Louisiana heat.

"The view is amazing. How far can I see?" Leia's enthusiasm was infectious as she stood by the wall and looked out over the city.

I laughed. "Well, we're not the tallest building around, but if you squint, you might be able to make out the glint of the Mississippi just over there. I have another casino I'm fitting into a riverboat." I rested an arm over her shoulder as I angled her in the right direction and pointed toward the river. Being so close to her was like a form of torture, and I had to stop myself from nuzzling her hair, holding my breath so I wouldn't lose control and take more than she would happily give me.

With my teeth gritted, I turned away and walked to the booth under the awning, barely looking up when she sat herself at the other end of the booth. Distance was good. Necessary. I needed to take this slow. Controlled.

"Chef has—" I started, but she held up a hand.

"Please don't say *prepared a range of dishes.* If your chef keeps cooking so much food, I might explode."

I laughed. "Not this time. I was going to say he's sent a traditional Cajun gumbo."

"Mmm." She moaned in appreciation before even seeing the food, and I was perfectly happy to keep feeding her in hopes of hearing that sound repeated.

Baldwin moved silently onto the roof and began serving our lunch, and as Leia took her fork in her hand, I asked my first question. I didn't need to

eat—it was something I only did for show, and not
something I enjoyed very much—so I tried to keep
myself busy with conversation while eating the
occasional mouthful so no one noticed anything
amiss.

"Did you grow up in Baton Rouge?" I knew the
answer, of course, but I was curious to see how
much she'd tell me.

Leia's reply was a harsh laugh. "Born here,
never even left the city limits." She laughed harshly
again. "Most likely I'll die here. Maybe even in this
casino if that look on your assistant's face earlier
was anything to go by."

I looked down to hide my grimace. I'd hoped
Valérie's attitude had passed her by, but maybe a
little instinctive wariness was a good thing. It would
help keep her safe around my family, who
definitely didn't share my philosophy on freely
donated blood rather than feeding directly from
the vein.

"Have you never traveled?" I kept the conversation moving rather than dwelling on Valérie.

Leia shrugged, a little defensive. "Haven't had much opportunity. Mom died, Dad went downhill, and I haven't even had time for friends or…" She stopped, and a pink blush flared across her cheeks. "*Friends*. So I don't really know how to be around people. Sorry if that interferes with your plans for arm candy. I'm more likely to be arm brambles, I suspect."

"That sounds…positively exciting. Do your thorns cause the good type of pain?" I murmured, and pleasure coursed through me as her blush deepened.

Her dynamic with Jean made a lot of sense now. As did her virginal status. She had no time for friends, let alone anything deeper, and she was obviously quite self-conscious about it. I moved the conversation away from anything that might embarrass her, spearing mouthfuls of crawfish and andouille between exchanging anecdotes and telling jokes just for the purpose of hearing her laugh.

"Do you mean it?" she asked after a while. Her eyes softened as she gazed up at me.

"Mean what?" I feigned ignorance.

She laughed and nudged my ribs gently. "You know what."

I shook my head. "Nope." I could still feel where she'd aimed that small nudge, like she'd seared it on me. I almost wanted to press my hand there and capture the touch forever.

She scoffed and shook her head. "You know what I mean."

I turned my gaze to her, looking deep into her beautiful eyes. "Yeah." My voice came out soft, deep. "Yeah, I do. And yeah, you are like your mother."

A lock of her hair fluttered around her face, and I lifted my hand to tuck it behind her ear before I froze. She watched me, her pupils dilating slightly, and I lowered my hand back to my lap.

She was quickly becoming the most tolerable human I'd ever met. And more than that, I wanted her in my bed for more than the power she'd grant me. Desire for her coursed through me, heating my blood.

As we talked more about her mother and Leia relaxed, she gradually moved toward me. Or I moved toward her. Suddenly, we sat very close together, our thighs touching, and I savored her body heat, not daring to move in case she realized we were so close.

The sunlight hit her hair and gave the deep brown a red glow, and something about her skin made me want to touch it. Stroke it. Lick it.

Pierce it.

My control was slowly slipping away.

I needed to taste her again. That kiss outside the store hadn't been enough. It had started a thundering desire inside me that couldn't be assuaged, and now my awareness of Leia consumed me in every beat of my heart, every breath I took.

At first, I tried to ignore it, but need rose inside me until I leaned toward her, close enough that my lips pressed against hers. So soft, so perfect, but she just sat there, and I waited. Then she pushed back against me, increasing the pressure of our mouths, and she sighed as she laid a palm against my chest, underneath my jacket but over my shirt. I groaned at the soft touch and slid my tongue carefully over her closed lips, willing her to open for me.

When she did, I explored the soft inside of her mouth, triumph like bubbles in my bloodstream. She'd welcomed me. This was *willing*.

Her tongue met mine with unexpected passion, and her rapid breaths increased my desire. I knew how she'd sound beneath me now, and it only made me want that even more. She moved her hand to wrap her arms around my neck, and her breasts pressed to my chest as she leaned in closer, eliminating the gaps between our bodies. We fit together perfectly.

But I'd known that already. She belonged to me, and we fit. As she shifted closer again, I took hold of her thigh and helped her swing her leg over me, breathing in deeply as the change in position released the scent of her arousal.

I couldn't think. I could only feel and move as she ground over my hard cock, rubbing the ridge of her jeans over it as she gasped out her breaths, and I kissed her in a frantic way I hadn't kissed anyone in more years than I could remember.

This woman stole my control as I ran my hands over her body, tugging her T-shirt free of her waistband so I could touch that soft skin. I drew circles on her back with my thumbs, and she moved faster against me like she was searching for something.

I wanted to give her everything, and I lifted toward her as she arched her back and her soft breasts pushed against me.

Her hands were in my hair, tangling, playing, tugging, and she murmured my name against my lips. *Nicolas.*

I inhaled sharply at the sound. She'd never said it before, and I wanted her to scream it as she came, for her to know she was truly mine.

I lost myself in her kiss, taking all she gave me, giving her everything she wanted.

But a shrill noise interrupted our moment, and Leia spoke against my mouth.

"I think that's your phone."

I sucked her lower lip into my mouth then nibbled on it, careful to control my fangs so they didn't descend, although my gums ached. "Ignore it." My words were a low command. "Whoever it is, they'll go away."

As if on cue, the noise stopped, but so had Leia. Her kisses were lighter, less passionate. She was withdrawing, and when my phone rang again, I growled but answered it.

I didn't even look at the caller display as I blew out an irritated sigh. "Yeah."

Then I helped Leia from my lap, my movements jerky and ungraceful before I walked out from under the awning like I just wanted a better view of the cityscape.

"Leave whatever it is you're doing," my uncle barked down the phoneline, and I tensed automatically at his tone. "You've picked up a spy. Someone from New Orleans is interested in your business."

"Fuck. I'll sort it," I snapped back, caught between ending the call and just tossing my phone over the building.

I hated bad news, and I especially hated bad news that interrupted a kiss like that. My body was still on fire from it as I shoved my phone in my pocket and strode back over to the table. My dick didn't know whether it was coming or going…well, really not coming. But it wasn't happy.

"We should get back downstairs." I tried to pitch my tone casual, but Leia's eyes widened and she ran her fingers through her mussed hair.

When she spoke, I couldn't tear my gaze from her swollen lips. "Are you okay?"

I nodded sharply. It was nothing she needed to worry about.

Once downstairs, I sought out Jason. "Something came up," I muttered, and Jason's eyes widened. "I need you to look after Leia. Spend some time with her in the casino, gamble a little if you can get her to do that. Tell her I'll be back for dinner with her."

I couldn't even look at Leia. If I did, there would be nothing to stop me pressing her against the nearest wall and testing for her arousal with my fingers, all of the people around us be damned. Even Jason wouldn't have been able to pull me off, and I trusted Leia's safety with him most of all. He wouldn't betray me by trying to claim her for himself.

Our human clientele was vaguely aware we had offices—security, camera room, my office, and the meeting room, and most of them didn't give two shits about those. The real action was on the casino floor for them. But for me, the real action happened underground, in the part of La Petite Mort humans wouldn't even dream about.

Fucking hell. I beat my hand against the wall as I walked, but there was no rhythm in it. Just fury. One of my subjects had been selling secrets to the New Orleans royal family, meaning they now knew information about the Baton Rouge royals that they could use against us.

Specifically about the virgin mate who would help me secure my rule. And that heated my blood and loosened my control for a whole other reason. No one endangered my mate and lived to tell about it.

No one.

And who the hell even knew? Who couldn't I trust? I'd find the fucker and deal with them, but not yet.

No, right now, I had something else I needed to take care of.

I thumped the wall so hard the plaster cracked and chips flaked away to land on the floor beneath me. I wanted to shout my rage, but that would just alert Percival that I was coming for him. My uncle had ensured Percival had already been brought in for me to *talk to*, but I had no idea why he thought he was here.

I shook my head. Fuck it all to hell. Now the New Orleans vamps would be all over Baton Rouge, trying to kill Leia or take her for themselves to secure their own future. It looked like my one-month timeline had just shortened.

My stream of curses grew in volume as I stopped caring whether Percival could hear me. His day of reckoning had arrived, and maybe he deserved to know that. And before I delivered his final punishment, I was going to tell him exactly why.

"Percival." I greeted him as I threw open the heavy wooden door to smack into the damp stone wall of his cell.

He took one look at my face and screamed.

Chapter 7 - Leia

My face burned as I followed along behind a younger guy with dark hair and an equally dark suit. Everything about him looked slightly deadly, even though he was shorter than Nicolas.

I touched one of my warm cheeks self-consciously. When had he become *Nicolas* in my head? Was that the effect of yet another of those drugging kisses? I lost myself when he kissed me like that. Let go and floated away, only conscious of his lips, his tongue, his hands on my skin, and my body pulsing with desire.

And I really had let myself go in his arms. I felt safe, and I felt wanted. But how far would I have gone? The memory of his body beneath mine, hard and ready, sent another wave of desire through me, and I inhaled a breath at how sharply I felt it. I'd wanted him inside me. Craved it, in that moment. But I barely knew him. Would I have gone so far?

I hadn't with any other man, and while I imagined the full romantic experience—soft lighting, and a kind, understanding man in a comfortable bedroom—apparently my body was A-okay with a bench style seat on a Baton Rouge roof terrace.

The fresh heat over my skin was less leftover lust and more embarrassment now. After all, I was fast abandoning the idea that being a twenty-eight-year-old virgin was a good thing these days. It wasn't something I generally told guys. The idea of purity didn't exist in our porn culture, and I hadn't been *saving* myself. Lack of opportunity definitely shouldn't be mistaken for lack of sexual confidence in this regard…although there was part of me where that confidence eroded daily. Being wanted was a powerful aphrodisiac.

That said, I wasn't about to jump on the first guy who came along.

Except I had.

Twice.

If Nicolas's phone hadn't interrupted us, what would I have let myself do? Would I have stopped? Stopped him? What would *he* have done?

I shook my head. Probably better I didn't know the answer to any of those questions. I'd said I wouldn't sleep with him, and regardless of whether he took that to mean actual shut-eye, I'd definitely meant sex. So that was that.

Except I was still so aware of him. His scent clung to my clothes. My skin felt branded where he'd brushed his fingers over me, his touch both teasing and purposeful.

I shivered just thinking about it, and Jason turned to glance at me, his eyes hidden behind dark glasses, his nostrils flaring slightly as he inhaled.

A slight smile lifted his lips. "You enjoy your lunch with Nic?"

I nodded, rolling the shortened form of Nicolas's name through my head. There was an intimacy in using it that wasn't mine to claim.

"Okay." Jason pushed through a door, and suddenly we were on the main floor of the casino. "I know Nic showed you around in here, but did he let you play anything?" Again, he half-turned, directing his words to me.

"Oh, I didn't want to." I had too many images of the tables Dad might have sat at while he squandered everything we had—fucking squandered *me,* even—to want to sit there myself. "All these people wasting their money? I don't know. It just doesn't look like fun to me." I shrugged, and Jason smirked a little. "I mean, no offense, or anything."

He chuckled. "None taken." Then he lowered his voice. "But you know, this can be fun. Not everyone plays to excess. It's supposed to be a game. But Nic will be the first to tell you the house always wins, and we do in the end. The important part for you to remember, for anyone who comes in here to remember, is that when the fun stops, you stop. The danger starts when people start chasing the next big win or try to make up what they just lost, when they've played what they *can't afford* to lose, you know?"

I nodded because shit, yeah. I knew about people playing what they couldn't afford to lose. "Sadly, I think I'm one of those things my dad thought he *could* afford to lose." I laughed but it didn't make my words any less raw.

"Yeah. Shit. Sorry." Jason sighed. "I shouldn't have said that. If it helps, though, I don't think Nic agrees with that philosophy."

Unexpected hope flickered in the center of my chest. But I extinguished it quickly. "I guess he just got lucky that I'm able to help him fulfil a couple of business-related commitments."

"I guess." But Jason's tone was noncommittal. Then he changed the subject. "Come on. Let me show you the blackjack table. If it helps, blackjack wasn't Jean's game."

I laughed again. "I think none of these were really his game, or I wouldn't be here, right?"

Jason blushed a little but he chuckled. "I guess they weren't." He led me to a table with a smiling dealer. "One more to play."

"No. I can't. I don't know how." I stopped before I sat down, strangely flustered.

"Ahh…a blackjack *virgin?*" The dealer raised one perfectly shaped eyebrow, and Jason glared at her.

"Cut it out, Sabine." Jason's tone turned commanding. Then he looked at me. "This is one of the easiest games. You start with one card and can request one card at a time from the dealer by knocking on the table. The idea is to get cards to the value of twenty-one or as close as you can. Closest wins. The number cards each hold their number value, face cards are worth ten, and an ace is worth eleven, unless that would send you over twenty-one, in which case it holds a value of one. Getting both a face card and an ace in your first hand is a blackjack."

"Okay," I said. "I can do simple math, I hope. But I have nothing to play."

"Nic has you covered." Jason set a pile of gold-edged black chips in front of me. They all stated the name of the casino and had the tiny heart logo in raised gold ink.

Sabine lifted both her eyebrows. "The boss has very deep pockets today."

"Really. Can it, Sabine," Jason growled almost under his breath. He took the seat next to me as she started to deal. "So, have you got any brothers or sisters?" he asked me.

I shook my head as I nibbled the inside of my cheek, trying to decide whether to ask Sabine for another card. Sixteen wasn't high, but it felt risky. Especially given I was playing with Nicolas's money.

"No, it's just me and Dad. What about you?" I was grateful for the distraction from the numbers.

Jason shrugged. "Not as far as I know?"

I narrowed my eyes. "Your dad…" I hesitated. Was I really about to ask if this guy thought his dad was a cheater? But how else would he not know if he had brothers or sisters? "Uh, was he *unreliable?*"

He coughed a laugh. "Not as far as I know. Pretty stand-up guy, actually."

"And Nicolas, does he have siblings?" I tried to drop my question in and still remain casual about it, but Jason's smile told me I wasn't as surreptitious as I thought.

"Yeah. He has… I think five, but they're all ma—" He broke off abruptly. "Adopted, I mean. None of them are his birth siblings." He looked away.

"Yeah, I know what adopted means."

Sabine laughed.

"Things with one of his brothers, Sebastian, can get quite…competitive. Nic's the oldest of all of them, though," Jason continued. "And he's… Shit. I don't know how old. *Old*, though."

I laughed as Sabine pushed more chips toward me. "*Old?* He can't be *that* old."

Jason's laugh was awkward. "Well, yeah. I meant compared to me. Everyone's old compared to me."

I glanced at him and shook my head. "Thanks. You're making me feel ancient."

"Who's ancient?" Nicolas's tone was light as he joined us, and I stiffened more from his hand on my shoulder than the hard glare he sent Jason's way.

"Me, apparently," I said. "Jason's been telling me how young he is."

"Scintillating, Jason." Nicolas's laugh washed over me, and I closed my eyes as the low sound seemed to vibrate deep inside my body. "Miss Boucher, would you do me the honor of accompanying me to dinner tonight?"

I glanced at my outfit. "I didn't really dress to go anywhere else." At Nicolas's smile, I amended my statement. "I didn't really dress to come *here*, I suppose."

But he shook his head. "There's no dress code at La Petite Mort. However, I can help you out with your dilemma. Come with me. Jason, cash in Miss Boucher's chips."

Flustered again, I turned to him as I looked at the small pile I'd amassed. "Oh, but they're not mine."

"Yes, they are." His tone brooked no argument, yet I tried.

"But the house always wins, right?"

He smiled, although it was more of a smirk, and he lowered his voice as he leaned toward me. "Sometimes I play a very long game."

My cheeks heated as Nicolas held out his hand. Sabine had busied herself preparing a new deck of cards, and Jason had already left the table.

"I've made an appointment for you at the boutique next door. And also the hair salon, if you wish." He spoke as if this was all part of our arrangement, and maybe looking the part was.

"Arm candy?" My question came out sharper than I intended.

"If you wish," he repeated. His tone was cool in response. "I do have an image to maintain when I'm seen in public."

Shit. I'd offended him. But what had I wanted him to say? That he wanted to spoil me? That I deserved some luxury in life? Fuck, no. This was a business arrangement, and I'd do best to remember that.

When I could keep my lips from his, anyway.

I lifted my chin and followed him from the casino. The boutique next door was a high-end one I wouldn't usually dream of going in. The women greeted Nicolas with air kisses before casting friendly smiles at me.

"Oh, she's perfect," one of them trilled. "What a dream to style." She turned to the other woman. "Should we go with the red? It will look gorgeous with her dark hair."

The second woman grimaced. "Mm…but maybe something to bring out her eyes instead?"

"I selected something for this evening when I called in and spoke to Romilly earlier, but how about both of the others as well?" Nicolas said. "Miss Boucher will need attire for tonight and a few more suitable outfits for future events. She also has an appointment at the salon for hair and makeup, if she'd like to make use of it."

One of the women clapped her hands together. "Perfect. We'll deliver her back to you evening-ready."

"I look forward to it." Nicolas smiled at me, his gray eyes full of the kind of dark promise that made my breath catch in my throat.

He left me alone with both women, who turned speculative eyes on me as they talked among themselves.

The excited one who'd clapped her hands turned toward the dressing room. "Let's see where Romilly put your outfit for this evening," she said. "You can start by taking a look at that before we check you in at the salon."

"Do you do this often? Style someone?" I couldn't hide the curiosity in my voice. Maybe Nicolas had an endless stream of women he dressed and styled like dolls.

"In general or for Mr. Dupont?" The more sedate woman watched me.

"Both," I said.

"In general, yes. It's our job. But for Mr. Dupont? No, never."

The excitable woman picked up the story again. "Although Romilly would do anything for him since he helped her when she was having all that trouble with her ex. Do you remember?" She glanced away as she received a glare from her colleague. "He was just so kind, and Romilly stopped being so scared," she finished.

I followed the two women into a delicately perfumed dressing area.

"Oh, it looks like Romilly left everything right here," one of them exclaimed, and my face flooded with sudden intense heat as my gaze moved right over a dress in soft gray that looked like it would fall to my knees in front and mid-calf at the back to a set of delicate lace lingerie in white.

"Mr. Dupont is a man of *very* good taste," one of the women murmured, and I was no longer paying attention to who was speaking.

All of my attention was focused on the clothing he'd selected for me to wear. Right down to the items no one usually saw. Except he'd know exactly what lay against my skin, what I wore under the beautiful dress. It was on the tip of my tongue to refuse. To pick something else out for myself. But with what money? I'd made a deal to spend one month with him. And part of me wanted to be the kind of woman—a beautiful woman—who wore clothes like these.

Hair and makeup was a whirl of activity that finished with me wearing a deceptively simple looking updo that revealed my neck but took more hairpins than I'd ever seen in my life to maintain, and I'd been given perfect smoky eyes.

The gray dress fit me like it had been tailor-made.

"Good taste and a great eye for sizing." Jealousy flashed fleetingly through the talkative woman's gaze, but it was quickly replaced by approval as she turned me to look at myself in the floor-to-ceiling mirror.

"Wow," I muttered. I wasn't sure even Harry or Pierre would recognize me. The dress was beautiful but not too much for a date in a restaurant. The lace and delicate beadwork across the bodice caught the lights but didn't overpower the fabric. And I didn't look like I was late to my own prom. I was understated but glamorous. Perhaps even worthy of a date with a high-rolling Baton Rouge casino owner.

The old-fashioned bell over the door tinkled lightly as Jason walked in, and when he saw me, he stopped, freezing almost statue still. Then he recovered and smiled. "I'm here to take you to meet Nic. Are you ready?"

The sensible woman inside me tutted and huffed a sigh under her breath, but the excitable woman too close to the surface spoke. "I can't believe you needed to ask."

Jason grinned self-deprecatingly. "I never assume." Then he turned to me. "Nic's waiting for you by the helipad."

One of the women who'd helped me get ready inhaled sharply, and Jason led me from the store, mostly ignoring my flurry of thanks to the two women. Just before I left through the door, the quieter lady handed me a gray pashmina wrap.

"In case you need it," she murmured. "Although with Mr. Dupont at your side, I can't believe you'll be cold."

***

Nicolas stood at the edge of the roof as dusk fell, his back to me as he surveyed the city spread before him. His hands were clasped behind his back, and he looked more like a shadow than a man in another one of his tailored black suits.

A sleek silver helicopter sat silently a short distance away. Well, it looked sleek to me, but I'd never stood close enough to another one to compare.

"Do you like what you're wearing?" Nicolas's voice sounded from right next to me, and I startled.

I'd been so busy looking at the helicopter, I hadn't even heard him move. Then my cheeks seared as I remembered he probably meant *all* the clothes. Even the lingerie he'd chosen. But I nodded. "Yes, thank you."

The back of his knuckles skimmed down the side of my neck from the bottom of my ear, and I shivered at his light touch as heat coursed through me.

"Are you cold? Let's get airborne." He approached the helicopter, and Jason appeared seemingly from out of nowhere and opened the door. Nicolas Dupont really did have staff for everything. There was probably even a guy who welcomed him into the bathroom and bowed gratitude on his way back out, or something.

I hesitated. "Where are we going?" I was about to get into an actual helicopter and fly fuck knew where with a guy who'd essentially won me in gambling debt.

"I know a nice little place in New Orleans." His face was partly in shadow, but the light caught his smile, and there was something disarming about it. "Let me show you the world beyond Baton Rouge?" He phrased it like I was the one doing him a favor, and I took a step toward him, beguiled by that idea.

I'd set my boundaries, but I was essentially at his mercy, anyway. If this was some sort of elaborate abduction, at least I'd go out on a once-in-a-lifetime experience.

I nodded as Nicolas held his hand out to me, and walked in his direction. His fingers were warm as they curved around mine.

"I've got you," he murmured, so soft I wasn't sure he was even speaking to me.

The inside of the helicopter was cramped with the pilot, Jason, Nicolas, and me inside it. Forget sleek. Apparently, my first impression should have been *small*. Nicolas drew the straps of my harness over my shoulders, then reached for the hem of my dress and bunched it a little as he delved quickly under the fabric between my legs.

I stiffened at the unexpectedness of his touch.

"Sorry." But he didn't look at all sorry as one corner of his lips tilted in mischief. "Only problem with a dress on a helicopter."

He fastened all five points of my seatbelt together and tightened it to his liking, then handed me a pair of headphones with a microphone attached and put a pair on himself before he fastened his own seatbelt.

The engines started, and the noise was loud, even with the ear protection. The pilot's voice crackled through my headphones, cancelling out the white noise, informing Nicolas of takeoff and flight duration, and then my stomach swooped as the helicopter lifted from the roof, the movement almost ungainly and uncoordinated.

I curved my fingers tightly around the armrests of my seat and gasped quietly. Then Nicolas's hand was over mine, coaxing my death-grip from the chair as he hooked my fingers into his again. When I glanced at him, he watched me without judgement.

"Watch as we approach New Orleans," he said, his voice soothing even over the communication system.

I glanced out of the windows, taking in the glints of water below us, and the silver strip of the Mississippi in the fading light. A bigger city sat ahead of us, lights starting to blink on as the sky began to bleed into pinks and oranges.

We landed in a way that felt every bit as gangly and awkward as takeoff, and my fingers tightened around Nicolas's. But now we were here, adrenaline spiked across my nerves for a whole different reason. I'd just completed my first helicopter ride, but my idea of a meal out was eating leftover fries in my office at The Pour House.

Something told me this was next level shit. Maybe Nicolas had made a mistake bringing me. This wasn't the sort of place I could fit in.

As if he sensed my apprehension, he touched one of the delicate curls they'd left loose right by my face. "Beautiful," he murmured.

Then I looked away as he released my seatbelt before helping me across the roof of the building we'd landed on.

"Welcome to The Neutral Zone," he murmured as he led the way into the restaurant.

***

We sat in a private booth with a perfect view of a small stage as a live jazz band played during our meal. Nicolas was a perfect gentleman—attentive without being overbearing—and I began to relax as each of the dishes he recommended practically melted in my mouth.

I looked around the red and black interior of the restaurant, and it was like some sort of representation of a lust-filled hell, which the sensual beat of the music only added to. Just as I started to relax, my body angling toward Nicolas, he set his napkin over the plate of food he'd only half-finished and flashed me an apologetic smile.

"There's some business I need to take care of quickly, but you're safe here." He stood as he spoke, not giving me chance to protest. "I'll be as fast as I can. Wait here for me, drink your fill, enjoy the music. I've taken care of the check, but I'll be back for dessert." He swept his gaze over me, something hungry and a little possessive in his eyes, and my body reacted to him straight away. Tension took hold of his face. "I won't be long."

I sat and listened to the music for a little while, taking in everything that made this space so different from The Pour House—and really, any restaurant I'd ever been to or imagined. The serving staff were smartly dressed and attentive. I only needed to catch someone's eye, and they brought me extra rolls or a fresh drink.

But I wanted more. I'd never been to New Orleans, and this seemed like a waste of time. I was sitting in a room while the entire city lay just outside. And Nicolas was nowhere to be seen. He'd probably want to leave as soon as his meeting concluded.

Eventually, the desire to explore made me restless. Nicolas had told me we were in the French Quarter, and I wanted to see all of the buildings I'd only ever glimpsed in magazines. As I sat alone in the booth longer, and the server's glances grew more sympathetic, I made up my mind.

If Nicolas was happy to leave me high and dry *again*—first a phone call during lunch and now what seemed to be a premeditated business meeting during dinner—I could take some time, too. And it wasn't like I hadn't run a slightly sketchy bar myself for years. I knew how to be alert and the types of people to watch out for. I'd had to learn how to judge people very quickly in my line of business and assess threat levels. I only wanted to walk down the street a little way, after all.

I wouldn't be gone for a long time. Just a good time.

I'd probably be back at the table before Nicolas was.

Chapter 8 - Nic

I walked away from the booth determined to return quickly. We were in the safest place in New Orleans, but nowhere was *truly* a safe place to leave my virgin mate. Not when she was the key to securing my reign and hadn't yet been claimed.

There were plenty of people in Baton Rouge and New Orleans who would either try to kill Leia to prevent me achieving the power granted to me by my birth or claim her themselves and remove me as a threat entirely. My blood heated in my veins at the thought of someone else taking Leia.

That wasn't acceptable, and I was here to make sure it didn't happen. And within The Neutral Zone, those threats were...well...*neutralized.*

Mixing business with pleasure wasn't ideal, but Percival and his attempts at subterfuge had made it necessary—I couldn't have him reporting back to Francois about Leia. I'd taken the right precautions—bringing us to The Neutral Zone, which guaranteed her safety as much as possible. She'd be fine in the restaurant for a little longer while I met with Francois.

I made my way up a grand staircase to the rooms upstairs. The red and black color scheme continued here, even more ornate, and it was like being in a whore's rotting pussy, regardless of Francois's delusions of grandeur regarding the regal atmosphere it projected.

Francois was heir to the New Orleans throne. He'd always been my peer in every way but age and experience—only my father had happened to die first, while his lingered in a stasis rumored to be caused by the slow descent into madness that seemed to run in the family. Francois ran The Neutral Zone as a safe place to conduct his political meetings, and generally, the clue was in the name. I'd never dared bring something as sought after as Leia through the door, though. I could only hope our negotiations here tonight would be worth the risk.

Leia was *mine*, and I needed the rest of the community to understand that—whether my mark was on her or not. And that included Francois. I was the only one in our position in possession of a virgin, and I intended to keep it that way.

I was here to stake my claim because vampires, especially young vampires, were like toddlers. If they saw something they wanted, they took it. So if I couldn't sway Francois with consequences regarding my ownership, I had something he might want almost as badly to secure his rule.

I hurried down a wide corridor. Crystal chandeliers hung above my head, reflecting and refracting hues of red like kaleidoscope droplets of blood, and a plush carpet beneath my feet cushioned my footsteps. Any vampire in the building would still hear me coming, though.

Leia's scent still lingered in my nose, solidifying my desire to return to her as quickly as possible.

I arrived at the door to Francois's office. Closed, of course. He'd want to start the meeting off in his favor—with me knocking like some meek subordinate for entry. And it wouldn't hurt me to play along, so I knocked. Like the good guest.

There really was no point in angering Francois when he already knew exactly what I had with me, the one thing that could secure either of our futures. Except Leia wasn't merely a virgin. She was also my mate. And that made her priceless. And *mine*.

"*Entrez!*"

I rolled my eyes at Francois's sharp command before throwing the door open, my gesture large and designed to take up space.

"Nicolas." He turned big brown eyes at me. He'd always struck me as a little insipid, possibly a little feminine, with hair that had been styled after a regency gentleman and his taste in clothes more flamboyant than my own.

But whatever worked for him. I wasn't here to exchange fashion tips like some fucking teenager.

"To what do I owe the pleasure?" Francois continued when I stood silently inside the door. He spoke heavily accented English, which was completely unnecessary because I wasn't sure he'd ever even visited France.

I sighed heavily, dramatically, *falsely*. "I'm afraid I'm here with bad news about Percival."

For a moment, Francois's eyes narrowed. Then he shrugged. "I'm not sure why you think I need to know about this Percival."

"He's no longer with us." I examined my nails. "Turned out he was a spy."

Francois gave a delicate shudder. "How unfortunate for him." Then he looked at me, his eyes cold. "But that doesn't explain why *you* are here, *mon ami*."

There was nothing friendly in his tone at all, and I scanned his gaze, tying to work out if the family madness had found him yet.

"To protect what is mine." I folded my arms, narrowing my eyes as I watched him.

Francois stood, his gaze reddening. "You came to my restaurant to stake a claim on something?" He advanced toward me. "You may have made a mistake."

His mild words didn't hide the sudden threat of violence emanating from him.

"The woman I'm dining with tonight—"

"*Oui*, the virgin?" Again, Francois sounded casual, but there was tension in the way he held himself. "She's a little *old* to be a true virgin, don't you think?"

But even Francois must have heard the lie in his words. There was no way he hadn't picked up Leia's scent. A hint of fang glinted as he smiled, and rage filled me. His fangs had descended while he thought of *my* mate?

"She is *mine*," I roared as I rushed him, grabbing his throat and pinning him against the wall, but he just chuckled lazily.

"Nicolas, Nicolas, Nicolas." He sounded so longsuffering. "If you were really staking your claim, why would you bring your new toy to play here?"

"My *new toy*—" I hissed the words "—means I can secure my reign as soon as I mate with her. You're still stuck waiting fifty fucking years until your father comes out of stasis—or is it getting longer each time, Francois? Does your father's death draw nearer even as we speak? Do you wonder if this time will be the time when he doesn't wake?"

He glared at me then seemed to remember himself and shrugged, the move careful and at odds with his red gaze. "As long as the woman you brought remains a virgin, it doesn't matter to me."

I squeezed his throat tighter. "You can find your own virgin and leave mine fucking well alone—and make sure your people do, too. I came to you to negotiate a political deal."

The red in Francois's eyes faded as he considered my words. He was always looking for new ways to stabilize his position without the protection of his father as king. As long as the king remained in stasis, Francois was vulnerable, a position I knew all too well. Anything that shored him up politically captured his interest.

"Ahh, but is anything you can offer me better than a virgin?" His tone was silky soft.

I nodded as I let go of his throat. "I believe so." I retreated a step back as Francois returned to his desk and pretended to look busy, even though his entire focus was still on me. "I've come to negotiate a truce."

"Really." The bored tone was back in his voice as he picked up a pen from the surface of his desk. He didn't even bother to make the word a question.

"A temporary truce, Francois. Don't sweat it." I goaded him like I would a sibling I'd grown tired of.

Our constant competition *did* tire me, but I also thrived on it. I just needed it to not exist right now. Francois smirked, and my temper rose again, but I gritted my teeth.

"Are you going to listen at all, Francois?"

"*Oui*." The word was a mere breath between his teeth as he waved a hand. "Continue."

"Leia is *mine*. She needs to remain mine until I have chance to claim her properly."

He shrugged like it wasn't his problem. "Oh, but Nicolas. We both know how I enjoy a hunt. The thrill of the chase."

"A month." I blurted the words as my control slipped. "For one month we won't interfere in each other's lives, and I will pay you for this agreement with that tract of bayou land you've always wanted."

The local shifter pack would be pissed at me for the deal, but Leia's safety was worth even their resentment. And the land got Francois's attention.

"And how many centuries has my family sought to relieve you of that land? All this time, it would have only taken one virgin?" He widened his eyes. "*Mais non*. Perhaps no one before now has needed any help to hang on to their virgin?"

He shook his head, the mock sympathy obvious. But instead of allowing him to goad me, I nodded stiffly, all of my muscles tense. Leia was too important to my future for me to fuck this up.

"The land you want in the bayou is yours for one month, free of interference by either of us in the other's life." I laughed, the sound empty. "Then we can return to our normal behavior."

It wouldn't matter to me after a month. I'd have claimed my virgin—my true mate—cemented my right to reign, *and* I'd have the power to defeat Francois and probably even reclaim my land.

I could have it all. But I still waited almost without breathing for him to decide.

And he knew what he was doing. He leaned back in his chair, and it shifted soundlessly under his change in position. He watched me for too long, like he was trying to make me squirm. The fucker. Final death was too good for him, but I couldn't afford a war right now.

Finally he nodded, just a gracious incline of his head as he rolled his eyes to look at me. "As you wish, Nicolas. As you wish."

Almost without acknowledging Francois's acceptance of my terms, I spun away from him and stormed down the hallway to return to the restaurant. That had taken way too fucking long, and he'd been a whiny little bitch about it, too. Couldn't he just be gracious for once in his fucking immortal life?

I jogged down the stairs and entered the restaurant, my gaze immediately on the booth where I'd left Leia. And it was empty.

The world seemed to slow, servers getting in my way as I sidestepped around chairs and other diners, like maybe I'd find her sitting where I'd left her if I just got close enough to inspect the seat.

But no. Still empty.

I slipped my phone out of my pocket and dialed Jason. I'd left him with the helicopter because a romantic meal didn't require my security guard and sireling as a third wheel, but what the hell had I been thinking? I'd left my virgin mate totally fucking unguarded.

Anything could have happened to her. I'd thought my presence in the restaurant and its reputation as a neutral ground would have been enough to deter any action against her—but obviously not.

"Jason." I barked his name into the phone when he answered. "Is Leia with you?"

He didn't answer yes or no. "I'll be right there."

My hand tightened around my phone at the words as I glanced around the restaurant again. I checked the ladies' room, walking right in like I owned the space, then the men's room, but she wasn't in either.

Jason arrived at my side.

"She's somewhere close, I can still smell her." Her light, floral scent was strongest at our booth, but it was elsewhere in the restaurant, too. "What if that bastard Francois…?" While I'd been upstairs, pursuing our deal, the deal he'd fucking *agreed* to—ah, but he'd made me wait. He'd fucking made me wait, the fucker. "What if he double-crossed me?"

Jason shook his head slowly, like he was considering the idea.

"I think I can track her. If someone took her, I can find her." I headed toward the doors. "Stay here and search. Don't leave any room out. If she's here, we need to find her. She's *mine.*"

I ground out the last two words, my jaw painfully tense. There was no fucking way I was leaving New Orleans without Leia. No way at all.

I pushed through the door onto the street, careless of anyone standing on the other side as I thrust it to bounce from the wall. I only had one thought in my head. Leia.

I inhaled deeply, trying to detect her floral scent, taking in the mixture of swamp, stale urine, vomit, and coffee before shaking my head and trying again.

My mate was here somewhere, and I'd find her. She wasn't safe on the streets in New Orleans by herself, and anger cleaved me that I hadn't protected her better.

Then it was there. Something delicate. Something floral. Something mine.

I darted between groups of milling tourists, their vision hampered by both the night and too much booze, losing then finding her scent again as different odors clamored for attention.

Suddenly Leia's scent changed, blooming into something bitter and acrid. Fear so strong I could almost taste it, and my gut became a tangle of knots. I picked up my pace, almost knocking people down as I pushed them out of my way. I had no time to go around stupid fucking humans who wandered into my path.

I needed to go through.

The scent grew stronger, and I focused in on three males huddled around my mate, caging her into a doorway. I watched as their eyes reddened, their fangs descending as they laughed and hands wandered over Leia's body. One dipped his head like he might bite her, fangs grazing across the delicate skin of her neck, and rage flared inside me. Primal rage tainted with something that tasted a lot like fear.

I roared my fury and hurtled toward them, intent on their destruction, my pact with Francois be damned.

Only Leia's safety mattered.

Chapter 9 - Leia

So many different sounds and smells surrounded me as I stepped onto the street and left the quiet interior of the restaurant. It would have been easy to get swept up in the crowds of laughing people making their way between bars and restaurants, but I'd long since learned how to move between drunk people while maintaining minimum damage to myself.

I glanced at the colors of the different bars, at the people spilling from the doors and the happiness that seemed to roll along the street like a wave. Snatches of foul smell were over-powered by cheap cologne and seafood. From somewhere, I smelled sweetness, like powdered sugar and beignets, and even after the meal I'd just devoured, my mouth watered in anticipation of tomorrow's breakfast.

Neon signs glowed in a rainbow of colors, and wrought iron filigree balconies packed with tables and chairs seemed to contain an impossible number of people. Their shouts and chatter echoed over my head as they leaned their heads increasingly close to one another to hear conversation while they occasionally cast their gaze on the busy street below, where I walked.

Maybe Nicolas would have liked to see this too. But truthfully, I didn't know what he enjoyed or if he wanted to play at being a tourist. It wasn't something in my contract. I'd only stepped out because I wanted to experience something in New Orleans that wasn't the inside of a restaurant. And if I only took a short walk and went back, Nicolas never even needed to know.

The little shops packed between the bars were closed now, but I drifted closer to the windows to peer at the wares. There were traditional tourist shops selling ball caps with bold slogans emblazoned across them and plastic pens and trashy keyrings that would break off in pockets or purses, but the one with the alligator eating the beignet made me laugh—it was the kind of thing I would have picked up for Harry or Pierre.

I moved along, stepping around a drunk guy emptying his stomach against the wall—apparently making room for more because the night was still young—and walked past the open door of a bar where the music was still jazz, but not the smooth kind that had accompanied my meal with Nicolas. No, this was raucous and almost made me want to dance, my muscles finding a new rhythm as I walked.

Something about the energy here seeped into my soul, and if my roots hadn't been in my rundown home and bar in Baton Rouge, I could maybe have seen myself walking this street as a local.

I wandered toward another of the tiny stores before recoiling slightly as the word *voodoo* caught my eye. Fascination drew me closer, even as a cold shiver worked through me at the multitude of skeletons in the window. Some of them were comical, but some of them looked downright fierce.

Perhaps it was a good thing the store was closed—I wasn't sure I could have resisted the allure of the unknown, even though the detectable thrum of power bade me stay away.

I turned from the store, ignoring the prickle at the back of my neck as I continued walking, heading toward a giant geode showcased in a third window. The energy here felt cleaner somehow, and my chest loosened as I blew out a deep breath. A range of pretty stones and gems gleamed from glass cases, and I allowed my gaze to wander over them—then took a step back as I met someone's eyes on the other side of the case.

The lady raised her hand and beckoned to me, her gnarled fingers crooking in indication that I should go inside.

The opening hours on the door stated that the store had closed long before, but when I pulled gently on the worn handle, it opened easily enough, and the scents of sage and patchouli raced out onto the street.

"You shouldn't be here." The woman's voice was cracked and as dry as her frizzy gray hair as it escaped the bun at the top of her head to wave in a wild mist around her face.

"Oh, I'm sorry," I murmured, sudden embarrassment heating my cheeks. "I thought you said to come in."

"New Orleans is very dangerous for you. Not safe." The woman tutted and reached out to touch my hair. "So pretty," she crooned. "Needs protection."

She darted across the tiny store with the rapid movements of a bird, her eyes bright, her hands already reaching toward one of her displays.

"Protection… Protection…" She muttered the word over and over again, one hand plucking various stones from the display before replacing them as she tried to smooth her hair back into place with the other hand.

I edged closer to the door and away from the obviously crazy lady. "Nice to meet you," I called. "I should probably go now, though."

This definitely wasn't where I'd planned to end up when I left the restaurant.

"Aha!" The woman snatched a purple stone like those that made up the geode in the window. It glinted a little in the low light. "Amethyst," she murmured as she clutched it in her palm. "But is it enough?" She looked back at me before nodding. "For now."

Then she pressed the crystal into my hand before cackling a laugh and withdrawing it to insert it into a cage attached to a thin silver necklace.

"Now, listen to old Lettie. This will keep you safe in the next part of your journey." She looped the necklace over my head, and the caged stone disappeared beneath my dress to nestle against my cleavage.

"Thank you. But I don't have…" Shit. I didn't have any money.

"You have need." Her eyes seemed to clear like she could focus again. "This old witch knows." She grabbed my hand, startling me. "And your future path is clear. I see great wealth, love, and power, but it's all shadowed by pain. And danger."

"Thank you," I said again as I moved myself from her grip. I didn't believe in visions and fortunes and bullshit.

The door blasted open behind me, but no one was there, and Lettie pointed a spindly finger, indicating I should leave. "Now go, but stay out of the shadows, child."

I half-ran back onto the street, the unfamiliar weight of the pendant heavy between my breasts. I almost removed the necklace, taking the delicate silver chain between my thumb and forefinger, but then I left it. I had no purse or pocket to carry it in, and there was something comforting about it that I couldn't quite place.

The store behind me was quiet again, and when I glanced behind me, there was nothing to indicate Lettie and I had been talking only moments before. It looked as closed as every other store in the street. I had no idea how long I'd been away from The Neutral Zone or whether Nicolas would have finished conducting his secret squirrel business dealings, but it was probably time to get back to the restaurant. Luckily, I'd walked in a straight line and not very far. I was too much of a magpie in places like this—attracted by pretty sights and color—which always slowed me down.

I looked at the sidewalk as I picked my way along the street and drew my wrap tighter around my shoulders as I walked as fast as I could back to Nicolas.

Only to stop abruptly when someone stepped into my path further down the street. My gaze skimmed from his heavy work boots to his dark, loose-fitting jeans and the two guys with him.

Something about them resonated trouble, and I started to cross the street, but a light breeze blew across me, catching my hair and teasing some of the loose strands. All three looked up as one, their gazes suddenly trained on me.

Shit. The air of danger increased when the one in the middle smiled, although *smile* was overstating it. The expression was little more than a cruel upturn to his lips. I hurried forward, suddenly clutching my pendant as my pace increased.

"I can do this, I'll be safe. I'll be safe," I repeated, like the words alone could make it so.

I started to run in the direction of the restaurant, but the guys caught up with me, using their bodies to maneuver me into a wide doorway so I could barely see into the busy street beyond them.

"Hello, baby." The guy clearly in charge brushed his fingers down my face, and I froze, fighting against closing my eyes because I couldn't just give up and not look. "Have you come to play?"

He leaned closer and murmured against my ear, his hot breath wafting over my neck. He smelled like booze and stale sweat, and I flinched away.

The other guys laughed, but one closed his fingers over mine. "Come play with us," he urged, his voice dangerously soft. "We like you."

The third guy had his nose almost in my hair. "Why do you smell so good?" he murmured, but it was clear I didn't need to bother answering.

But for fuck's sake. Had none of these guys heard of shampoo or soap or basic personal hygiene? I tried to stand on my tiptoes to see beyond them, but a hand rested on my shoulder to press me back down, and I lashed out with my foot, landing a kick on his shin.

"Play nice now, little honey," a voice said, and it was like I hadn't even touched him.

I tried again, kicking out, and attempting to jerk away from their holds. But nothing I did had any effect.

"You smell amazing." The one with his nose against my hair had a fetish or something.

I tried to work out a plan, because being raped on the street was not going to be the end result of this trip to New Orleans. It couldn't be. I'd dealt with dicier things at the bar...but Harry and Pierre had always been there, just in case. My vision blurred at the sudden thought of the two guys who'd always protected me without seeming to think about it. They were just always there when I needed them.

And now Dad had gambled me away to Nicolas. Someone far less reliable, apparently. Someone who had actively brought me somewhere really dangerous, if my current situation was anything to go by.

Beyond the three men, laughter still rang out in the street, but I couldn't make a sound. My voice was lodged like a stone in my chest. I could barely breathe around it.

The leader nuzzled against my neck. "Mmm… I can smell her master, too." He lifted his head. "Why hasn't he claimed you yet, darlin'?"

Holy crap, the guy was on drugs. My fear turned cold. He was high as a kite, obviously. There'd be no reasoning with him. Shit. Maybe they all were.

One of the others laughed roughly. "Must be our lucky day, finding such a sweet treat wandering the streets."

The third one laughed too, his nose still in my hair. "The perfect dessert. I could die happy just smelling her."

I gritted my teeth. They were pissing me off. They weren't doing much more than smelling me, but I'd taken a shower today and I wasn't wearing perfume. I huffed a sigh and started to push forward, trying to work my way between them, but the leader pushed me back, slamming me against the wooden door.

"That's not nice, cher. Why're you leaving so soon? We're not finished. Stay and sample proper New Orleans hospitality." He grinned maliciously as he grasped my thigh, digging his fingers in like he might rip a chunk away.

I sucked in a fractured breath, and his grin widened.

"Even her fear is sweet." He inhaled deeply, and there was the unmistakable sound of a zipper.

"No." I found my voice as I tried to push through them again.

"Hold her," he growled, and as I watched him, his brown eyes blazed to red, like two jewels shining in his face.

I took a breath to scream, squeal, shriek… *anything*, but one of the men pressed his hand over my mouth.

"Make sure she can breathe," the guy with the red eyes and his hand down his pants commanded. "I prefer them conscious."

"Hurry up, though. I want my turn." The third guy, who'd turned his back and appeared to be keeping watch, laughed. "But I don't care if she's conscious."

I expected to cry or try to scream or fight my way forward again, but I stood, numb, and watched as the men discussed me like I wasn't even there. The guy who'd had his hand down his pants stood in front of me and bent toward my neck, his breath mostly alcohol fumes.

"Where to pierce first?" His words were a murmur as he grabbed me between my legs. "This untouched pussy or her pretty little neck?"

"You're killing me," the guy with his back turned said.

"I vote neck." The guy with his hand over my mouth spoke, and his eyes glowed a dim red, too, but surely that was wrong.

One of the neon signs nearby must have been casting the light. Or I'd had too much to drink at the restaurant. That would also explain my slow reaction times. Usually, I was a fighter. But the more scared I became, the less I seemed able to do. The man with his hands on my body drew back and grinned, and I gasped, jerking my head back so it slammed on the wood behind me, sending pain lancing through my skull.

Fangs.

Holy shit, his teeth had grown, and he had *fangs*.

With a malevolent chuckle as I made a list ditch struggle, he bent to my neck, and his warm breath was followed by the scrape of teeth. I couldn't even think. My mind had nothing left to give.

As he waited, those impossible fangs resting lightly against my skin like he was savoring something, there was an inhuman roar, and a shadow whirled in front of me, ripping the man away from me. I collapsed to the ground without anyone keeping me on my feet, and the other two men stood for a moment before a flurry of curse words colored the air and they ran away, their out-of-rhythm footsteps echoing the pounding of my heart.

Before my eyes closed, the whirlwind of a man who'd dragged my attacker away took off after the escaping pair and took them both to the ground. But before I could see what happened, my eyes drifted closed, and I almost ignored the footsteps beside my head. It was so nice just to rest.

No. That was wrong. I forced my eyes open again as adrenaline pumped through me. I couldn't collapse on a street in New Orleans. Those guys had already shown me it wasn't safe.

"Miss Boucher?" At Jason's familiar voice, I finally gave in and let myself drift away.

Chapter 10 - Nic

I'd never known rage like this. It consumed me completely, and rational thought became impossible. I acted on instinct, turning my fury into brutal revenge as I methodically destroyed the men in a back alley, turning them into a pile of unrecognizable body parts before I finally stopped, exhausted but still on edge.

Then I only had one thought.

Leia.

Fear flung me into motion, and fear wasn't something I was familiar with. People were afraid of *me*, but *I* was never afraid. Only now I was. What had these fuckers done to Leia? Was she still alive? Had I been too late—had one of them drawn blood and claimed her?

My throat dried at that thought. I stood to lose everything because of my own stupidity. I never should have brought Leia here. An unclaimed virgin? My mate? I hadn't even fucking claimed her, and I'd trusted other vampires to abide by rules of honor and respectability? *I* was the dumb fucker. Total fucking screw up. And I'd fucking believed fucking Francois.

Fuck.

I exhaled a hissed breath as I raced back to where I'd left her. The image of Leia almost getting fed on—maybe even about to get her throat ripped out by little New Orleans vampires— was still front and center in my head. And I hadn't been there. I'd misplaced my faith when I put it in Francois, and I wouldn't make that mistake again.

More than anger, something territorial clutched me, something… I hesitated, almost unwilling to identify it. Something *protective*. But then I shook my head. Of course, I was protective—my whole fucking future depended on not letting Leia get killed or claimed by anyone else.

I arrived back where I'd left Leia to find Jason kneeling protectively at her side. No one was really paying much attention to one more passed out person on the streets of New Orleans, especially with Jason right there. He definitely gave off the air that he had the situation all under control.

"How is she?" I all but skidded to a stop next to them.

He patted her hand. "Mumbling a bit. In and out."

As if she'd heard my voice, her eyes snapped open, and she started to scream. The sound began quietly but grew louder and higher pitched until I leaned over her, looking into her eyes.

"You need to sleep," I murmured. "Sleep and forget this."

As I spoke, repeating the soothing words, her scream died away, her eyes closed once more, and her tense muscles relaxed.

Shit. I was an asshole. Using compulsion on my mate? But I didn't know how else to calm her. She didn't trust me yet, and I needed her mind whole. She'd just seen literal monsters, ones she shouldn't even know existed. They'd almost killed her, and I couldn't let them live in her thoughts. She needed to sleep. Both sleep and to *forget* as I'd commanded.

"I need to get her back to the helicopter." I reached for her, but Jason lifted his hand.

"Uh, you've got something on your face, Nic." He made as if to point out where on his own face then just made a circular motion over the whole thing. "Kind of…there."

I lifted my finger and swiped it down my cheek. It came away slick and red. "Well, shit." I couldn't exactly go marching back through The Neutral Zone carrying my mate and wearing the blood of my enemies.

I wiped the sleeve of my jacket over my skin, but Jason shook his head.

"I think you're just making it worse." He stood and shrugged his own jacket off. "Here, swap with me. I'm on clean up duty anyway, right?"

I nodded. "Although it wasn't meant to go down like this. You get rid of the bodies. I'll take

Leia home." I looked at her face and an exhale gusted out of me, regret both uncomfortable and unfamiliar. "I shouldn't have brought her. But what were my options? I only trust you with her, and I needed you with me. Give me a call when you're done here?"

He grimaced, sucking in air between his teeth. "How many pieces did you leave them in?"

Leia groaned.

"Oh, putting them back together would require an instruction manual and tools." My words were for Jason, but my attention was entirely on Leia.

Jason stood from his crouch and shrugged his jacket off before handing it to me and taking my blood dampened one in return.

"We're very lucky you favor black clothing," he grumbled.

I ground my teeth a little as I looked at Leia. "She's wearing gray, though."

"Be careful how you pick her up. Keep her held against you in case there's blood transfer." He shrugged. "Vampirism should come with a how-to guide."

Usually, Jason's ridiculous comments amused me, but not right now. I reached for Leia and drew her into my arms, settling her against me. I'd have to walk through The Neutral Zone, and Francois definitely had cameras, but he also knew I was protective of Leia, so this shouldn't look too odd. Or I could just say Bourbon Street had been too much for her. I slipped her shoes off and let them dangle from one of my fingers, like any man trying to make his mate comfortable.

"Call me." I flung the words over my shoulder as Jason melted into the shadows and I strode toward the restaurant, the most vital thing in my life in my arms.

I didn't take the main door into The Neutral Zone. Every diner in the place didn't need to see Leia asleep as I carried her. I took a side entrance closer to the stairs that would eventually lead to the roof instead.

And I took those steps two at a time, ignoring cameras that turned lazily in my direction as I moved. I would have given one a casual wave, but I didn't want to change my hold on Leia.

We reached the helicopter without incident, and the pilot opened the door.

"Too much fun on Bourbon Street," I murmured, guilt festering inside me at the casual lie.

I settled Leia into a chair, buckled her in, and set headphones over her ears. Then I sat beside her and took her hand without even thinking about it, stroking my other hand over her fingers so they wrapped around mine. My arms felt empty without her in them, and my heart seemed to have an irregular beat as I studied her face, so devoid of movement.

My gaze wandered to her pale neck, to the two red scrapes there, where the vampire had teased her with his fangs instead of biting down. Only luck separated my current relief from what could have been grief, and that was like a punch to my gut.

It was a situation I hadn't controlled.

A thin silver necklace gleamed against Leia's skin, and when I plucked at it, I withdrew a caged amethyst pendent from beneath the fabric of her dress. Was this the reason she'd left the restaurant? Sightseeing? Shopping? So much risk, for nothing.

Concern, equally as unfamiliar as regret, gnawed at me, and by the time the rotor blades stopped spinning after we landed on La Petite Mort, I'd already made contact with Jenkins and Baldwin, so they'd be ready.

Jenkins met me at the private entrance to the casino, and I settled Leia into the limo then ran quickly inside to change into some spare clothes in my office.

When I reached the limo again, Jenkins open the door so I could slide in alongside Leia. I studied her face, looking for any discomfort or changes.

"Has she moved at all, or spoken?"

Jenkins shook his head. "No, sir."

She didn't move on the journey back to the house, either. I carried her through the hallway and up the stairs, Baldwin alternately flapping behind me and springing forward to open doors. When I laid her on the bed, and a smear of the blood that had transferred earlier from my shirt onto her dress became visible, Baldwin gasped.

"Master, does Miss Boucher require a doctor?"

I shook my head. "It's not her blood."

"Shall I send Emma to assist you?" He gestured vaguely between Leia and the bed.

Protective instincts claimed me again—no one should see my mate like this but me—but I pushed them down and nodded. "That might be for the best. When Emma arrives, I'll take care of some business before coming back to check on Le…Miss Boucher."

Baldwin nodded. "Very good, master." And he left the room, his rapid strides audible even on the plush carpet.

***

In my quarters, I grabbed a quick drink, threw myself under the shower, and dressed in a clean shirt and pants. Black to suit my mood. I grinned weakly at my own pathetic joke. Black suited my mood every day. It was all I owned.

My cellphone rang just as I stepped through the double doors and bent to lock them behind me.

I glanced at the caller display. Jason. "Yeah?"

"Dealt with." He used as few words as I did on the phone, and I didn't ask what he'd done. The bayou was nearby. And alligators were always a convenient excuse for a shredded body or three.

"I need you to see Francois." I'd thought about it on the way home.

"Smelling like three of his dead minions?" Jason rarely challenged me, but I continued telling him the plan anyway.

"The helicopter will meet you at the airport. Too risky to use The Neutral Zone helipad again, I think."

He made a murmur of acknowledgement.

"But Francois needs to know our deal is off."

"Fuck, Nic," Jason ground out. "Then it would definitely be too risky for me to try to hop on the chopper on his roof. And you want *me* to deliver this message? You sure it's not just a suicide mission? Might not need a chopper at the airport after all."

I nodded as I looked over the balustrade to the hallway below, my fingers reflexively tightening and loosening around my phone. "You're there, I trust you, and more importantly, Francois knows I trust you. He'll know if it's coming from your mouth, it's ultimately coming from mine. And he wouldn't dare try to hurt you." I ground out the last words, believing them and hoping they were true at the same time.

Jason sighed.

"The deal is off. The truce no longer exists. The bayou land remains mine. I can't trust him. My mate couldn't even walk down the street safely in Francois's territory." My stomach clenched over the fact she shouldn't even have been out there. If she'd have just stayed in the restaurant as I told her to, I'd have taken her anywhere she wanted to go.

My sudden vehement thought surprised me. But it was true. I would have taken her anywhere, bought her any trinket that caught her eye.

Jason sighed again. "I think you should—"

"Not interested in what you think." I snapped the words out as my concern narrowed into irritation. Worry for Leia had become claws buried deeply in my chest, and each breath I drew in dragged them deeper.

A clock ticked on the wall behind me as I listened to Jason's regular inhales. Finally, he spoke again. "Maybe wait a few days. Make a decision then." He left off the fact that this was the thought I'd just told him I didn't want to hear, but my phone screen still cracked worryingly under my tightening grip.

"That's your suggestion for my next move, is it?" My voice was soft, almost a purr, but Jason's reply was strong.

"Yes, it is. Don't burn a bridge you might need to come back across. And how could Francois let everyone know so quickly? How would they know about the truce?"

I barked out a harsh laugh. "Francois burned down the bridge and the whole fucking town the moment my mate was attacked in his territory by vampires under his control. He's lucky New Orleans is still standing. He needs better behaved subjects." I boomed the last words out and they echoed inside the cavernous two-story space in my home. Then I glanced behind me at the open doors to the east wing and lowered my voice. "Just make sure the message gets through to him, Jason. I was serious about protecting Leia when I spoke to

Francois earlier, and I'm *fucking* serious now. No truce."

"Okay." Jason's tone said he still didn't agree, but he knew better than to continue to argue.

"I'll send the helicopter to the airport. Call me when you get there." Even though he could be stubborn and a little resistant sometimes, his safety was still one of my top priorities.

"Okay. Talk to you soon." He hung up, and I swung around, my thoughts already back with Leia as I covered the distance from the top of the stairs to the guest wing.

I hesitated outside her door, unsure whether I should enter her private space, given privacy had been one of her negotiations before agreeing to spend a month with me.

But how could I protect her if I wasn't there at her side? It was where I needed to be.

I'd never felt a pull like this before, and I rested my forehead against the door for a moment as I sucked a deep inhale, but it didn't help. Her scent pervaded my senses. She was everywhere, all around me.

I opened the door, and it whispered across the carpet before I crept in and moved the armchair from the sitting area to beside the bed. I sat down with a heavy sigh that seemed to well up from somewhere around floor level and focused my gaze on Leia's face.

Unable to stop myself, I leaned forward and brushed some loose hair back from her cheek. Emma had taken out the pins holding her hair in place, and it rested loose around her shoulders. Hopefully the gray dress had gone to be cleaned, although that was the least of my worries. I could buy her a new gray dress for every day of the year if she'd liked it. And I would, if that was what she wanted when she woke up.

"Hey." I spoke softly. "I am so sorry about today."

The words were out of my mouth before I even thought them.

I didn't apologize. I didn't get things wrong.

But today I had.

Today, I'd fucked up so badly, I'd nearly lost my mate.

Maybe I needed to tell her the truth about me, about vampires, about those fucking New Orleans freaks, so she knew exactly how seriously she needed to take her safety. But then what?

Then I'd be scary. I'd be something out of a horror movie.

And no one went willingly to the villain in a horror movie. I would put everything with Leia at risk if I told her now. I hadn't spent enough time with her yet to convince her I was worthy of making my claim. Unless she accepted me, I'd just be a monster.

I didn't want to be a monster to her. Fate was drawing us together, but she needed to *fully* accept me, to give herself to me, or… Fuck. I needed willing blood, willing surrender of her body, and I couldn't risk what little trust I might have built between us.

She shifted a little in her sleep, and a small crease appeared between her brows. I ached to smooth it away or to know what had caused it. A murmur drew my attention to her lips, and I longed to feel them against mine again.

I took her hand between my palms, and I was the willing one. Willing her to wake because I needed my mate.

My queen.

Chapter 11 - Leia

I rolled over, not quite ready to wake up but also not still sleepy enough to drift away again. I tucked my nose back under the thick comforter and prepared to just rest, but something in the luxurious room felt different.

Something was out of place.

It was completely quiet, but a presence lingered on the periphery of my mind. I didn't feel alone, and I slowly opened one eye, finding myself peering through slightly blurry vision at Nicolas, who was sitting in a chair close by, revealed by the half-light making it past the edges of the curtains.

I stifled a gasp and opened the other eye, then just watched him for a moment. He didn't move; his eyes were closed, and his chest rose and fell steadily. It was safe to surmise he was asleep and unaware of my perusal. Well, scrutiny was more accurate than perusal, especially with the way his unbuttoned shirt revealed the beginning of a tattoo over his left pectoral muscle.

He was still in last night's clothes, and tousled was a good look on him. I hadn't really taken an opportunity before now to study him closely, but this was like a free pass. He actually looked peaceful without the usually-present lines of tension around his mouth and eyes. Sleep had smoothed him out.

I shifted and bit back a groan as my body protested the movement, a series of aches echoing through me. When had the truck come rumbling through the bedroom and run me over?

Had I had too much to drink in New Orleans? I could just about remember the restaurant, but then things got a little fuzzy. Why was Nicolas here looking all rumpled and uncomfortable…and actually kind of sexy?

That tattoo drew my attention again. It disappeared under the black fabric of his shirt in the most tantalizing way. Made me want to follow it…with my tongue. I closed my eyes against the unexpected thought and the image it conjured.

Carefully, quietly, so the rustling covers didn't disturb him—and so none of my movements hurt—I shifted my legs until I was sitting on the edge of the bed. Then I held my breath as uncertainty seized me. What the hell was I thinking?

For a few moments, I just sat and watched Nicolas, and lust unfurled lazy fingers low in my abdomen. My gaze wandered to his tattoo again and again, the dark ink against his skin more tempting to explore than I'd have believed possible.

I flicked my tongue over my lips and stood, reaching behind myself to the mattress as I found my balance. Releasing a long, slow exhale, I waited some more, convincing myself he'd wake and find me watching him.

But he didn't, and my desire to know what his tattoo was overrode all of my misgivings and my common sense. I took a step closer, between his spread legs, and I rested my palm on the chair behind him as I gently teased the open front of his shirt from his body.

Then I frowned. It was a shield and some sort of… I squinted, taking in the delicate lines that formed a…fleur-de-lis, only it was so ornate, the top petal almost resembled a vulva. And below that delicate script drifted across his skin. *Ego So…*

"Good morning." His low voice seemed to vibrate through me, and I let go of his shirt as my knees buckled and I sat in his lap, directly on his right thigh.

My breath whooshed out of me, and his arms wrapped around my waist until we were face to face and he opened his eyes, suddenly pinning me with a soft gray gaze. And it wasn't stormy like usual. It was gentle and comforting.

"Shit," I gasped. "Fuck. I… Sorry. I'm sorry. I—"

The corner of his mouth lifted in an amused smirk, and his arms tightened almost imperceptibly.

Too close. He was too close. Oh, fuck. I burned for him. My body was on fire, heat whipping over my skin and right through me, my clit pulsing like a second heartbeat.

I pressed my hand against his chest to push away, create some space between us, but his body heat seared my palm. "I…" But I had nothing to say. I wanted to do bad things to this man, and my throat dried as I imagined all the places I wanted to touch him and him to touch me, and I looked away in case he saw all of that in my eyes.

One month. That was the contract I'd signed. Just one month. And I'd been the one to state no sex. There could be no sex. No *bad things*, no matter how needy my body turned out to be.

My fucking traitorous body.

But I sucked in a breath, hoping to find both oxygen and resolve in the air. I just needed to keep up my end of the deal. One month. Then I'd be free and clear. Homeowner, business owner, and able to reclaim and rebuild the legacy of my family. Of Mom.

My future was so close I could almost touch it. I couldn't ruin it.

Nicolas began to draw circles on my back, and despite myself, I relaxed against him, craving more of his touch.

Wanting *him*.

I wanted his hands lower, on my ass. Higher— on my breasts, teasing my nipples. My eyes slid closed, and I parted my lips, barely smothering a moan before it escaped and revealed too much about my state of mind.

When I looked at him again, his eyes were almost sleepy, and he watched me, his gaze kind and expression unguarded. I leaned in closer as if there was a magnetism between us that I was powerless to resist.

Shit. I needed to get up.

Like, I *really* needed to get up, not lean so close to Nicolas that our lips almost touched.

But I couldn't.

I waited, not even a breath away, without knowing what I was waiting for. Or what I was hoping for.

I shouldn't have been hoping for anything.

He pulled back a little, and I didn't know whether to sigh in relief or disappointment. Then his fingers touched my neck as he brushed my hair over my shoulder and looked at my skin. A shiver ran through me.

"Do you remember anything from last night?" His voice was low and soothing.

I tilted my head. "It's all a bit fuzzy." That was an understatement. I could barely remember a thing. A sensation here and there, Nicolas's face, but nothing else.

He grinned, but it was endearingly lopsided as he swept hair from my forehead, his eyes not quite meeting mine. "You had a drink or two too many and danced the night away. I spent most of the night watching your body sway to a beat only you could hear."

His grin lifted a little, but heat burned my cheeks.

He chuckled softly, his gaze suddenly searching as he looked at me, then he leaned forward and pressed a soft kiss to the corner of my mouth. Immediately, I wanted more, but he was gone, already changing his position to clutch me against him as he stood.

Practically against my own will, I snuggled against his chest, not finding the words to say anything before he lowered me carefully to the bed. I helped him draw the banket over me, ignoring the way my body still hummed with awareness for him, and I pressed my thighs together, but that just made me want him more.

"I need to shower and get ready for work." He kept his voice low. His tone was almost regretful, and I couldn't look at him because if I did, I might invite him to stay. Or to use my shower. With me inside it.

He walked to the door, and I made an artform of not directly watching him. But I was aware of every movement he made. His fingers curled around the door handle, and he half-turned, not quite looking at me as he spoke. "We have a party to go to tonight. It's formal. I'll send people to do your hair and makeup."

Just when I thought he was about to leave, he spoke again, like he'd remembered something. "Oh, and Jason will be your guard until further notice."

"What?" I lifted my head off the pillow. "Why?"

He waved a hand dismissively. "Oh, no real reason. Just had some trouble with a couple of clients who don't like some of my rules. Extra precautions, and I'll have it all ironed out soon."

I nodded. Spending time with Jason didn't bother me, and I planned to get some more sleep anyway. I was suddenly really tired again. I allowed my eyes to drift closed and couldn't quite keep the smile from my lips as Nicolas closed the door behind him. His scent lingered all around me from where he'd held me against him, and it comforted me.

When I finally woke again, showered, and changed, I left my room and Jason pushed himself off the wall next to my door and fell into step behind me.

"Good morning, sleeping beauty," he muttered, and a loud stomach rumble punctuated his sentence.

I covered my mouth. "I am so sorry. I had no idea you were standing out here. Haven't you even had breakfast?"

"Nicolas told me to guard, and I can't guard you from either of the dining rooms." He didn't sound disgruntled—just amused.

I huffed a sigh as I descended the stairs, my hand trailing on the smooth, wooden bannister. "Seriously? We're in Nicolas's house. I think you could have had your breakfast, though, especially as I believe Chef is making beignets this morning."

"Sounds good to me. *Any* food sounds good to me." Jason lowered his voice. "It's been a while since I've eaten."

I glanced back at him, and his eyes caught the light in a way that made them glow a little red.

Mr. Baldwin stepped forward from his position by the dining room. "Miss Boucher." He nodded at me. "Jason."

I stopped. "Have you all just been waiting around for me to get out of bed?"

Mr. Baldwin smiled faintly then gestured into the dining room. "I'll let Chef know you're here."

Breakfast was a lazy affair, although watching Jason eat was funny. It was like he didn't do it often and he'd forgotten how. Baldwin approached him with a drink, and I raised an eyebrow.

"Wine for breakfast?"

Jason huffed a laugh. "Hardly. After being on guard duty most of the morning, I need an energy recharge with a super berry cordial."

I wrinkled my nose. "Think I'll stick with coffee."

And immediately Mr. Baldwin was at my side, offering me a refill of coffee like I'd never tasted. It was smooth and dark and had an almost caramel taste. I was going to be well and truly spoiled after a month of drinking this coffee and staying in this house.

But as I thought of home, my heart lurched. I missed the people there. "What's Benedict like?" I asked suddenly.

Would he be good to my people? I almost laughed at the thought that Harry and Pierre were *my people,* but I'd pretty much gone ahead and adopted them as uncles—whether they wanted that or not.

Jason took another sip of his drink then nodded. "He's a good guy. Like me, Nic trusts Ben with all aspects of his life—including what belongs to him."

He gave me a slightly pointed look, but irritation flared in my chest.

"The bar will soon be mine." Only a month. I just had to stick this out for a month.

Jason swallowed again then dropped his napkin onto his half-finished beignet. "What's next? You have some time before you need to be party ready. Movie? Video game? There's a cinema in the basement."

"Popcorn, too?" I lifted an eyebrow.

Jason chuckled. "You just ate breakfast."

I laughed too as I stood and tucked my chair under the table. "I know, but popcorn can persuade me to do pretty much anything."

"I'll be sure to let Nic know that." Jason's words floated over his shoulder as he headed to the door.

"That and pizza," I called, and Jason rewarded me with another chuckle.

"Noted."

We spent the rest of the morning combing through Nicolas's extensive movie collection, barely watching anything except for the odd scene here and there as we compared our favorite movies and Jason did bad impressions of various characters.

Lunch was pizza delivery, and I laughed. "Beignets, popcorn, and pizza. Fantastic."

Jason smiled. "I think the party later might be better than slumming it here with pizza and a movie. Nic's family knows how to throw a party."

I froze for a moment. His *family*? I'd thought maybe business associates. Hoped for that, anyway. Family felt strangely intimate. But he'd mentioned that in our negotiations, so I shrugged it off. I could handle a bit of family.

"Will you be there?" I asked. Weirdly, Jason was the closest thing I had to a friend in this big, museum-like house. "This morning has been a lot of fun."

Jason's eyes were gentle. "You won't need me there to guard you while you're with Nic, among his family."

But his words were hesitant and seemed to be laced with apprehension, and that sent a shiver of forewarning through me, reigniting the desire I'd felt when I first arrived here—the one that made me want to know more about Nicolas Dupont so I could release myself from the deal.

If Jason thought Nicolas's family was dangerous, that meant Nicolas was likely dangerous too. I'd become too relaxed since I got here. Too focused on lasting the month when I could probably break the contract earlier and still get what was promised to me.

My mind wandered to the perpetually closed doors of the west wing, but before I could ask Jason anything, Mr. Baldwin appeared.

"Miss Boucher." His usual clear tones rang across the room. "The stylists have arrived, and

I've requested they set themselves up in your suite."

"Thank you." I turned to wave at Jason, but he was already on his feet.

"I'll come and stand outside your door again," he said by way of explanation.

I waved him away. "Oh, you don't need to do that."

"Nic said I do." His face was expressionless, and there was clearly no point in arguing with him, so I turned to leave again, Jason trailing behind me.

Upstairs, my room was a flurry of activity. One lady was setting up makeup on a table, and another was plugging in various tools for styling my hair. A third woman popped her head out of the huge closet and squealed when she saw me. "Ooooo! She's here! Isn't she adorable? This is going to be so much fun!"

A smile crept across my face, awkward and halting at such enthusiasm and attention. Part of me had hoped to slip into my room almost unnoticed, but that hope was quickly gone as the other women started to speak.

"Hair or makeup first?" The lady with all the styling devices held up a curling iron.

"Bathroom," I murmured. "Want me to wash my hair?"

I grabbed a robe the woman in the closet held out to me, and at a nod from the hairdresser, I escaped behind a locked door. This was a lot. It was almost too much. Aside from last night, I'd never spent more time in a salon than it took to trim a couple of inches off the bottom of my hair, and even those visits were irregular.

When I walked back into the bedroom, the robe wrapped tightly around me, the hair stylist beckoned to me. "Hair first," she said. "Are we doing loose with big curls or up?"

I sat in her chair, and she played with my hair, forming it into a twist and lifting it into a pseudo updo before her gaze drifted to my neck.

"You know what? I think those big loose curls might work nicely, after all." She quickly positioned some rollers and turned on the hairdryer, removing the need for conversation as she teased my hair and positioned it just how she wanted it.

"You must be such a temptation," she murmured as she worked. "I wonder what the family will say when they meet you?"

"She was certainly the talk of the casino guys." The makeup artist giggled.

"Yes, well, they know the rules. Nothing too *challenging*." The hair stylist shot her an odd, warning look and the makeup artist glanced away, suddenly busy examining the label on a small pot of moisturizer.

I studied my fingers as I twisted them in my lap, hiding my expression from the women in the room. What *rules*? It felt like everything that was said around me was spoken in some sort of code. What was Nicolas involved in? For the second time of the day, I pictured the west wing doors. The only place I wasn't allowed to go. Those were *my* rules apparently, the ones I had to follow.

But perhaps I could choose not to. Next time I was left alone, maybe I could ditch Jason if I needed to and find my way in. It wasn't like the guy followed me to the bathroom.

The hair stylist proclaimed me done soon enough, although she couldn't resist a last teasing touchup of a few of the curls before passing me to the makeup artist. For the second time in as many days, I looked flawless. That had probably never been true in my life before.

And when the stylist emerged from the closet, practically humming a fanfare as she walked toward me, an incredible dress in her arms, I didn't know what to say.

"Holy shit, that can't be for me." Yeah. I *really* didn't know what to say, so I just blurted out words.

The women with me laughed. "Nic has really good taste, right?" The stylist lifted an eyebrow, but I remained silent.

"He chose *you*, you know, so your answer should always be *yes*." The makeup artist put her lotions and potions away as she spoke, and I pulled a face she didn't see.

If calling in a debt was *choosing*, then yeah.

But I didn't say anything. I simply watched as the stylist laid the dress on my bed and then produced another fancy lingerie set, this time including thigh-high stockings. Holy fuck, I was going to look like a porn star under my dress. Thank God high-rolling casino owners and their families didn't come equipped with X-ray vision.

Self-consciously, I lowered my robe, my hands shaking a little as I revealed my body to three women I didn't know before stepping into the new panties and allowing the stylist to fasten and position the bra just right for under the dress. Then

I drew the stockings on before she could even attempt to help with those.

She picked up the dress and held it out for me to see, and I swallowed against a suddenly dry throat. It was a beautiful shade of emerald green, with a structured bodice, nipped-in waist, and tiny black crystals that had been stitched in a floral pattern and glittered as they caught the light.

"I think I'll look like a queen," I blurted.

"Nic's queen." The makeup artist sighed dreamily as she leaned on the vanity, her hand cupping her chin as she watched me step into the dress.

The bodice was surprisingly modest, only just revealing the swell of my breasts, but it was backless, and the stylist reached into her bag.

"Just one last thing." She produced a necklace studded with what looked like tiny rubies and which had a huge ruby-colored pendant dripping from the center of it. She motioned me closer and fasted the clasp at the front of my neck so the pendant hung between my shoulder blades and the smaller gems glittered all the way down the base of my neck, looking for all the world like tiny droplets of blood.

"Stunning," she whispered as she motioned her finger for me to do a twirl.

I glanced over my shoulder to a floor-length mirror. Wearing a necklace backward wouldn't have been something I would have thought to do, but the unexpected effect of it against my skin was incredible.

"You're ready, Cinderella." The makeup artist choked on a giggle, and the hair stylist shushed her and sent her yet another warning glare.

"We hope you have a lovely evening, Miss Boucher," the hair stylist said, her voice so reverent I almost expected her to curtsy.

I made my way to the top of the stairs, pausing with a hand on the bannister as I glimpsed Nicolas below, staring upward expectantly. When he saw me, his lips parted and his eyes widened. As I walked slowly toward him, his gaze seemed to wander all over me, practically searing through the dress, and heat flashed over my skin as electricity sizzled between us.

When I reached the hallway, he stepped toward me, his gray eyes molten with desire, although his face held the tension of a predator. It wasn't a look I'd inspired in men before.

My chest tightened as I tried to inhale, but I was caught in some kind of spell. Nicolas's spell.

"Like the dress?" I asked, trying to sound casual, but my voice cracked, and my chuckle became sharp as he leaned toward me, his breath warm against my ear.

"I've never seen anything as beautiful," he murmured in low words meant only for me. "And you tempt me to forget the party and remove that dress right here so I can see the rest of you." He moved back again, his gaze still hot and hungry as he watched my face.

I opened my mouth to reply, but there were no words. I just breathed out a small puff of air as lust wound delicate threads through me, tightening into a coil low in my belly, and I grew wet with need.

Mr. Baldwin cleared his throat discreetly from the corner, and Nicolas grabbed my hand, suddenly galvanized into action.

"We need to go before I fuck you on the hardwood," he murmured.

Chapter 12 - Nic

Holy fuck. Just the sight of Leia in the dress I'd selected… I'd known it would be perfect. And whoever had given her that necklace… My blood hummed through my veins just at the sight of the red around her neck where I wanted my teeth to pierce her delicate skin, where a thin trail of blood might escape to. I wanted to gather drops of her blood with my tongue as she writhed with pleasure beneath me.

She smelled divine—her scent, the power in her blood called to mine. I hadn't been able to keep myself from telling her what I wanted to do to her. The very sight of her fogged my mind, making my existence and movements dreamlike.

The world slowed around me, but I had to act. I took her hand to lead her to the limo, although the idea of being in such a small, enclosed space with her… I shook my head as my dick jerked against my pants.

Fuck. I wasn't ready for an assault on my senses like this one. Touching her was almost painful, and I fought to override my base desires. I wanted to drag her somewhere—anywhere—and take her, savor that first bite. Hell, I wanted her under me on the hardwood floor as I brought her pleasure.

I couldn't have chosen a better bride if I'd been searching for her myself. And fuck, I didn't believe in fate, but here Leia was. Almost fucking *presented* to me, and perfect in every way. All that strength, all that power… So much possibility.

And tonight, she was giftwrapped. I wanted to tease off every layer, to unwrap her and reveal her smooth skin to my hands, my lips, my tongue. I wanted to graze my fangs over her neck. I wanted to pierce her and plunge my cock into her.

I wanted all of her.

Every last movement, every last moan.

I wanted my name on her lips and I wanted it all now, to feel her power coursing through me, claiming me as hers as I claimed every part of her as mine.

Thoughts of that first bite drove me almost wild with need, and I stared ahead at the waiting limo, thinking of what we were doing tonight, what I could achieve by attending the party and indulging in the first public showing of my virgin... My mate.

But now was also the time to be careful. I wasn't only showing how I'd claim my full power; I was revealing my hand.

I breathed in carefully, not daring to glance at Leia, holding my control tight around me like armor. I'd never been so close to the edge.

I greeted Jenkins with a stiff nod and reached to hold the car door instead of him as Leia moved in front of me, protectiveness surging through me at the proximity of another male, which was ridiculous—my staff was selected based on their absolute trustworthiness.

Still. Leia was *mine*.

Once in the car, I raised the privacy screen immediately to keep her just for me, but as much as that pleased me, it also trapped me with her. I glanced at her, then again, and I could smell her arousal, the exact same as this morning when I'd wanted nothing more than to thrust up into her waiting body to satiate the hunger and need for both of us.

I gritted my teeth against the urge to drag her across my lap, but when I looked at her again, she turned a nervous gaze in my direction like she sensed my wild desire for her.

"You look beautiful." My words came out raw, almost gruff, around fangs that ached with their need to descend.

She blushed, her skin taking on a light pink shade even in the low light of early evening, and the sight of that blood so close to the surface thickened my cock. I almost groaned, and she leaned toward me, the movement slight, but I missed nothing as I watched her.

She lowered her eyes, the movement submissive and demure as her lashes fluttered against her cheeks, and I gave in to the desire to touch her. Just my fingers on her skin wouldn't hurt. A mere shoulder. Something safe.

But then she lowered her eyelashes and they fluttered against her cheek as she exhaled, and it undid me. My simple touch turned into a lazy swirl of my fingertips over her skin, a circle growing larger until I brushed the column of her neck. She gasped, and the swell of her breasts rose, her skin pebbling in tiny goosebumps against my fingertips, her desire telegraphing itself.

"I didn't want to leave this morning." My words were part apology, part bold statement, all low and rough. "I wanted to stay and fuck you."

Leia gasped, and I leaned forward and flicked my tongue against her lips, stealing a taste as the scent of her arousal filled the back of the limo. *I'd* done that. My virgin wanted me, and I wanted to crow my victory. I wanted to taste her all over, too, and I dipped my head to touch my lips to the neckline of the dress.

She was a walking jewel and deserved worship.

She touched my hair, displacing strands of it in tentative movements as I let my hand rest on her thigh, waiting a moment before I started gathering the fabric and moving the hemline upward. I held my breath as I waited for the first touch of that soft, forbidden skin.

"*Nicolas.*" My whispered name on her lips was an aphrodisiac meant just for me, and I slid the material faster, though careful not to ruin it, as I continued my quest for a touch. Just one touch.

Something to assuage the hunger burning in my chest for this woman.

But one touch would never be enough. I exhaled a shaky breath as I brushed her skin, relief mixing with anticipation of more. Sheer fucking *raw need* of more.

I waited a moment longer, allowing her to adjust to the new sensation, completely still as I fought not to turn to my head and plunder her mouth. Then her legs parted a little, just a fraction—the smallest of invitations.

"*Nicolas.*" Again, that whisper. Only this time it meant so much more. And the invitation was so much bigger.

I skated my hand between her thighs, and her breasts rose and fell without rhythm as she sucked in shaky breaths that she puffed back out against the side of my head. Her panties were damp, wet with her desire, and I turned my head to look at her.

Her gaze met mine, her green eyes almost liquid as she watched me, and I wanted to give her everything.

"Let me..." I whispered, my lips almost against hers, but I waited for her small nod before I kissed her.

She quivered beneath me before her arms wrapped over my shoulders, her hands pressing the back of my head and neck, holding me close as my tongue teased the seam of her lips and my finger slid under the edge of her panties, delving between her folds.

"Mine," I murmured, and her breath caught as I circled her entrance then brushed over her swollen clit.

She arched against me, her hips lifting.

"Good girl." I whispered encouragement. "Already so greedy."

I touched her clit again and nudged a fingertip inside her. A strangled sound emerged from her throat, and I waited.

"Okay?" I wanted to please her, to pleasure her, not scare her, and I waited for her nod before I pressed further in.

"*Please*, Nicolas," she panted, but her eyes were wide like she didn't quite know what she wanted as her hips continued to move.

"Nic." The sound almost rumbled through me. "Call me Nic." I wanted all of her passion, all of her intimacy. "And you are Leia."

I drew my finger out of her a little then plunged it back in, enjoying the small cry of pleasure trapped between our lips. I moved again and stretched my thumb to strum against her clit, setting a rhythm for her body to obey.

I followed the same rhythm, moving with her, unsure who commanded who, who *drove* who, as my cock sought friction against my pants, and I groaned against Leia's lips as my tongue swept into her mouth. Her breathing grew increasingly ragged.

So close… So close…

"Leia… Leia…" I whispered her name. A command. An enchantment. A mantra. My whole body moved against hers, my cock nudging against her outer thigh, mirroring everything I wanted to do over her, inside her, as I teased myself.

Tension entered her muscles and she stiffened against me as she sucked in a breath and the soft walls of her pussy pulsed around my finger, the strong tightenings sending a bolt of desire through me as I continued moving, gentling and slowing to ease her down.

Her breath came in little puffs, and a blush returned to her cheeks as I slipped my finger from her body and rearranged her panties. I straightened her dress and chuckled, and her gaze met mine.

"Oh." Her teeth pressed briefly against her lip. "I mean, thank——"

I pressed a finger to her mouth, not interested in embarrassment-driven gratitude. "There's so much more," I murmured. "So much more. And I'll do it all for you later."

She nodded once, the movement sharp, and she didn't flinch from my gaze. "Okay."

Surprise stole my voice at her reply and her attitude, and my cock stiffened painfully, the hardest I'd ever been. I brushed my palm over my pants, teasing myself further as my other hand lingered over the controls to the privacy screen. I really wanted to turn the car around, go home, and claim my virgin.

But Jenkins's voice came clearly over the speaker. "Arrival in two minutes, sir."

And my opportunity vanished as quickly as it had presented itself. I took Leia's hand in mine. "You ready?"

She exhaled a long breath. "To meet your family?" Her eyes flashed with amusement. "Never."

I grinned in response, then froze as her fingers touched my cheek.

"You should smile more." She looked thoughtful, but before I could lean into her touch, selfishly taking more of her for myself, she withdrew and looked out the window.

The countryside here was denser, less built up with human habitation, and if I rolled down the windows, the sweet, soft air of the bayou would drift in, bringing with it the green smell of vegetation and growing things.

I leaned back as I entwined Leia's fingers with mine before bringing our joined hands to sit on my thigh, teasing myself as much as comforting myself with her proximity. Fuck, I missed that wild Louisiana smell and the memories it held.

I'd known this area since it was little more than jungle, with nature in full control, and being back relaxed me as the feeling of being *home* filled me. I breathed easier as I basked in memories of the past and considered all my ancestors had seen and done here.

But returning here as the new yet unconfirmed king… That was different.

We turned onto the long driveway of my ancestral home, where my father had ruled from. The mansion was set back from the road. To anyone else, it would have looked like another country road, one of the many that maybe only locals used, but to me, this was home. Ancient trees lined our way, their branches dripping with Spanish moss that shone silver when the headlights flashed across it. Occasionally the tips of the foliage kissed the roof of the limo, and my hearing picked up the soft swish of the fronds.

As we approached the house, every window seemed to glow in welcome, and people hurried in the main door, alighting from vehicles that formed a slow train around the wide circular driveway. A fountain sat as an ornament in the middle, and Leia almost pressed her face to the glass to look closer as naked Venus bathed in full view of passersby.

Someone had strung fairylights between the trees up here, and they twinkled a delicate welcome.

I leaned forward as Jenkins joined the line of cars, waiting for our turn to get out of the limo and join the party, and my hand tightened protectively around Leia's. This was both a moment of great triumph and a moment to be cautious. I needed to make my claim known.

When Jenkins drew to a smooth stop, I slid from my seat and held out my hand for Leia to join me. Her eyes widened, and she hesitated at the edge of the seat, her gaze travelling to the house then up as she took in the vastness of the building, the stately columns that rose for two stories, and the wide balcony that spanned the front.

"Your family lives here?" Her voice was little more than a whisper.

"Yes." I leaned forward, making my next words conspiratorial. "It's a bit of a fixer-upper, but they're happy."

She caught her breath and looked at me then narrowed her eyes. "Fixer-upper, my ass. This place is perfect."

I nodded an acknowledgement as pleasure tightened my chest.

"You're perfect." The words slipped out, so quiet I almost hoped she hadn't heard them, but her gaze flicking briefly back to mine told me she had.

I wanted to give her all of this. Perfection. Riches. Power.

She deserved nothing less, and the wonder on her face hurt my heart because she'd clearly never experienced the life she was meant to have.

This life.

As she accepted my hand, I froze. Her fingers felt so natural against mine, but when had this one human broken though my *all humans are annoying* barrier? I wanted to make her smile, to hear her laugh at the things I said and moan my name at the things I did to her body. I wanted to claim her, own her...keep her. But I didn't quite understand *why.*

"Are you all right?" Her voice was soft, hesitant, and awoke me from whatever spell she'd managed to cast on me.

I nodded a sharp acknowledgement. "Always. Just thinking about tonight's business."

Her lips tugged down for a moment like she was disappointed, but she quickly recovered.

"Arm candy." She smiled, but the expression didn't reach her eyes as she tucked her hand into the crook of my elbow.

I patted her hand briefly as she reminded me of the terms of our contract. A companion for one month. A contract we'd already broken when I finger fucked her in my limo, my driver on the other side of a privacy screen, but if this made her entrance into my family's home easier, I wasn't about to argue. She was at my side, and my fingers still carried the scent of her body and her desire.

Those two things were all that mattered.

My mother's butler, Owens, greeted us just inside the wide front door, and as he roved a glance over Leia, he hesitated. I shook my head in the smallest of movements. No title tonight.

He lifted his voice above the quiet chatter. "Nicolas Dupont and guest," he announced.

The room stilled, the atmosphere shifting to something predatory and aware as heads swung in our direction. Nostrils flared as curious gazes landed on Leia.

I rested my hand over hers again, the movement deliberately possessive and designed to see off any challenges. As my father's rightful heir and their new king, my people needed to respect my status and my obvious claim.

The electricity of watchfulness still crackled in the air, and I moved my hand to the small of Leia's back, resting my palm against the skin bared by the cut of her dress as I walked toward my mother. Mother stood alongside my uncle, my father's brother, with a group of friends and elders from our people but looked up as soon as I approached with Leia.

Like their attention had ever really been anywhere else. They were just better at appearing disinterested.

"Mother. Uncle." I inclined my head respectfully as I greeted each of them. It hadn't taken long for my uncle to come sniffing around in the vestiges of power—offering his protection, no doubt.

"Nicolas." My mother's eyes widened as her gaze travelled to Leia. "And...?" She half-gestured toward her.

"Miss Leia Boucher," I supplied, my hand still possessively on Leia's skin. I tucked her closer to me as she held out her hand to my uncle.

"Pleased to meet you." Her voice was clear but quiet, and I drew small, absent-minded circles on her back with my thumb. Reassuring myself or comforting her, I wasn't quite certain.

"This is a surprise." My uncle's voice was loud, and I tensed my jaw as he took Leia's hand, his huge palm swallowing hers. It irritated me that he had no discretion, and also that he was touching her when she wasn't his.

Mother leaned toward me for her customary air kiss, but her lips lingered near my ear.

"The one?" she whispered. "Your virgin?"

I nodded.

"Good." Then she drew away, her eyes sparkling as she looked over Leia again. "You're a pretty little thing," she said, and Leia's cheeks flushed pink.

I rolled my eyes. Of course, Mother knew she was more than pretty. There wasn't one person in here who hadn't picked up Leia's scent, although I was probably the only one who knew she was my true mate, so maybe no one could guess her actual power or the power she could unleash in me, my ability to hold my throne and rule absolutely.

As Mother and my uncle continued to watch her, Leia fidgeted a little, her fingers twisting together in front of her. I waited to see if they had anything further to say, but apparently not as they returned their attention to their friends, probably to engage in conversation I wasn't ready for Leia to hear just yet. Mother looked like she might burst if she couldn't announce to someone that Leia was *the one.*

"We'll go and get some drinks," I said, and spun us away from my mother's tight group.

The bar was across the room, and conversations fell silent as we passed, whole clusters of people stopping everything they were doing to watch us pass by.

"Is everyone okay?" Leia kept her head facing forward, but her gaze darted from side to side like she was aware of the unusual scrutiny but didn't want to address it directly.

I grinned. "Yes. It's unusual for me to have a…" I hesitated. There were so many things I wanted to call her. "A companion, that's all."

"Really?" Her steps faltered as she looked up at me. "I'd have thought you would…"

"What?" I grinned as I met her eyes.

She shrugged. "I don't know. Been *popular?*"

I laughed as we reached the bar, and the hired bartender gave us his attention immediately.

"Sir?"

I ordered our drinks and returned my focus to Leia. I'd just lifted my hand to tuck a lock of her hair behind her ear when someone grabbed my hand right out of the air and pressed it to a pair of soft lips.

"Nicolas!" A familiar voice caressed my name, and I gritted my teeth as I turned to my left.

"Aurelia. Nice to see you." Except it wasn't. It never was.

She stood to the side of me and ran her fingers down the lapel of my jacket like she was straightening my clothing for me. Her touch was possessive and unwanted.

"I've missed you," she purred, and Leia took a step back. Aurelia leaned forward, her lips nearly touching my ear as she spoke. "I'm still waiting for my proposal, Nicky." She flicked out her tongue and swiped it over my skin. "You know I'm destined to be your queen."

I closed my eyes briefly so Aurelia wouldn't see my irritation there. She'd always been a gold digger, desperate for my family's money and prestige, desperate to be my queen. But she didn't fulfill any of the criteria to allow me to secure my place on the throne, and there was nothing captivating about her.

My gaze slid to Leia, drawing Aurelia's attention there, too. Her eyes widened and her nostrils flared, and she stepped toward my mate. Aurelia opened her mouth as she prepared to snarl, but I spun her back around before she could bare her fangs.

"Raylie, calm yourself," I growled. Then I looked at Leia. "Wait here for me and don't move." I had to contain Aurelia's threat before it got out of hand.

Leia parted her lips, but I turned away, my hand around Aurelia's upper arm as I drew her to the other side of the room. I glanced back at Leia, and she was sipping her drink, her gaze darting around the room. No one else was near her, though, which was good.

"What are you doing, Nic?" Aurelia wrenched away from me.

"*Nicolas.*" I emphasized my name. She didn't deserve the intimacy of *Nic.* "You need to get yourself under control. Leia doesn't know what we are, and I need to keep it that way for the time being." I kept my tone low, my voice urgent. I didn't want to waste too much of my time talking to Aurelia, but I needed her to understand.

She folded her arms and tapped her foot. "Oh yeah?"

"Yes," I hissed. "And if you don't comply, I'll take away everything that holds value for you—including your access to high-level vampire society."

I held my temper in check, aiming to look bored as I spoke to her. If she knew how important this was to me, she'd act against me out of sheer spite.

"Okay." But she agreed too readily, the shrug of her shoulders too simple as her eyes shone with a familiar malice.

Fuck. I'd have to watch her. Aurelia was dangerous when she was on a mission—especially when she thought she'd been fucked over. Dammit. I curled my hand into a fist. I didn't have time to contain Aurelia as I needed to. I had to get back to Leia.

"Just behave," I ground out before I turned back to where I'd left Leia.

I strode in her direction, but she wasn't there. I arrived at the bar and glanced around, but she wasn't standing anywhere nearby. I walked through the room, then even out into the garden where some couples stood and chatted, but she wasn't there either.

This was all far too familiar. I should have spotted the pattern ahead of time: I took Leia out with me, left her alone, and she wasn't there when I returned. Perfect.

Fuck. I scrubbed my palm over the back of my neck as I turned a full circle, searching for the splash of vibrant green that would tell me I'd located my mate. But she wasn't anywhere.

Fear was a slow, creeping prickle as it worked through me, and I inhaled slowly. I wasn't used to feeling afraid. I never feared anything. I was protective of what belonged to me, but being territorial was different than being fearful.

And I didn't know what to do with that.

I stood straighter and pushed the uncomfortable fear aside. Leia was mine, and someone else had her, and I was fucking well going to find her. Then I'd deal with the person who'd dared extend such a direct challenge. Another wave of anger heated my blood.

I took a deep breath, hoping to clear my head so I could think. I tapped as many guests on the arm as I could, ripping them from their conversations because my need was greater, and I ranked above them.

"Have you seen my companion?" The word felt so dry when she was my mate, but I'd publicly shown my claim. I didn't want to endanger Leia by declaring just how important she was.

Without exception, people shook their heads. I was just heading to the bathrooms to check there too when I caught a trace of Leia's floral scent lingering in their air. I followed it out of the ballroom.

I was going to rip the fucking head off whichever fucker she was with. No one took what was mine.

Not anyone who wanted to live and tell about it, anyway.

Chapter 13 - Leia

I watched Nicolas walk his friend across the room. *Friend.* They'd seemed closer than friends. His girlfriend, most likely. And that was shit. I swallowed a mouthful of whatever alcohol the bartender had provided for me and grimaced. I shouldn't have cared, but I did, and that particular truth was a bitter one.

But if Nicolas already had a girlfriend, what the hell was I doing here, being paraded around like a fucking dress-up doll and introduced to his family? And what the fuck had that been in the car on the way over?

My cheeks flamed at the memory, embarrassment stronger than desire now. How many times was I going to let Nicolas leave me to my own devices while he was off taking care of whatever business he had going on? Family business, actual business, personal business… It didn't matter. I didn't need to be there for any of that shit. It was just a power play, and I was getting damn tired of it. I slammed back another drink. I didn't even know who the bartender had set it out for. That didn't matter either—as long as it burned my throat on the way down and made my eyes water.

I watched Nicolas and his friend where they were on the other side of the room. She was perfect. The epitome of gorgeous—even with my hair and makeup and a personal stylist, I couldn't rival her. I didn't have a cute little French accent, for one thing.

Nicolas stepped closer to her, and I didn't need to see what happened next. I looked away, a sudden mess of wounded ego and hurt pride as he bent his head toward hers. I'd thought he was giving his kisses to me, but maybe I'd thought wrong.

Holy shit, *of course* I'd thought wrong. No one took possession of someone for a month—

especially someone who'd categorically stated she wouldn't put out—and didn't seek attention elsewhere. Our arrangement didn't *mean* anything to him. I'd been foolish to think otherwise, even just for a moment.

Didn't mean I had to watch, though.

I slammed my glass down on the bar hard enough to rattle the other glasses sitting nearby before I surveyed the room. I'd never been to a party like this one, where the guests were refined and genteel, where laughter tinkled rather than boomed rowdily, and where the music was twiddly notes on a piano or violin rather than pounding from a jukebox or someone's cell phone and speakers.

My dress was something else, too. I'd never been this dressed up. I wasn't like the women Nicolas was obviously used to. This was a big deal to me—I looked like something out of a fairytale. And I was here in this wannabe-castle with a whole group of people I had nothing in common with, but I could definitely still walk around the room and enjoy myself. I'd never get this opportunity again.

I started moving slowly, almost creeping around the edge of the room like I was afraid to be there, like I shouldn't have been there, but then I gave myself a shake. Hell yes, I deserved to be there. I'd fucking been claimed to be here as part of a gambling debt. If Nicolas didn't want me to mingle, he shouldn't have brought me. I didn't need to sneak around in the shadows.

A warning about shadows lurked in my mind, but as quickly as I thought it, it was gone.

I lifted my chin, avoiding eye contact with every crazy in this room who seemed determined to look at me—I certainly got more attention from the party guests than I got from Nicolas, which was both interesting and even more of an ego crusher.

But I was more than happy to show him how little I needed his brand of attention, where *anything* else going on seemed to be more interesting than spending time with me.

"Hello."

I looked around at the first person who'd dared speak to me. Up until now, I'd only been watched, like I was the mouse in a room full of hungry cats all content to bide their time. The man looked vaguely like Nicolas in the same way Jason did, all broad shoulders and self-confidence, but he smiled more easily, a huge grin already on his face as he looked at me.

"I'm Sebastian Dupont." He held his hand out, but when I put mine in it, he drew my fingers to his lips instead of the greeting I expected. His mouth brushed my knuckles, and my skin flushed with heat. "I'm Nicolas's younger, far more desirable brother." He dropped his voice conspiratorially and winked.

I giggled, startled and surprised at his bold flirting after Nicolas's hot-or-cold attitude.

"Pleased to meet you," I murmured, not quite holding his gaze.

"And it's truly a *great* pleasure to meet you," he replied, and his broad chest swelled as he inhaled deeply. "Nic appears to be otherwise engaged."

He made a vague gesture of his hand in the direction of where Nicolas had taken his friend, and I fought the sudden surge of rejection that gripped my chest.

I hadn't been rejected. I'd been brought as arm candy only, and he could talk to anyone he wanted. Even if I seemed to be the arm candy Nicolas sometimes wanted to fuck. I ignored the little voice in my head that pointed out that arm candy actually belonged on someone's *arm,* so maybe I wasn't even *that,* and returned my attention to Sebastian and his apparently permanent grin.

"Can I step in for my shockingly inattentive brother and offer you a tour of the house?" He held his arm out for me to take. Oh yes. This brother seemed to know about arm candy, too.

I hesitated, but only for a moment before I slipped my hand into the crook of his elbow, the same way I'd allowed Nicolas to escort me into the house. And I ignored the cramp in my stomach. I'd wanted Nicolas to show me the house, really, but that was stupid. He didn't need to include me in his life, and I was really only being nosy. Anyone could show me around. Perhaps I'd even pick up some tips for the eventual refurbishment of my own home—something that would have made Mom proud.

"Thank you." My voice was still low, and when I chanced a glance at him, he was gazing down at me with a mixture of curiosity and longing.

Then he blinked and it was gone, so maybe I'd only been projecting what I actually wanted to see on Nicolas—which was definitely an idea I needed to get out of my head, or this would be an even harder month than I'd originally anticipated.

Sebastian and I walked around the edge of the room, almost sticking to the same shadows I'd stepped between originally. I glanced around, searching for Nicolas, but I didn't see him. He was probably still talking to his friend. I pushed away the tendrils of jealousy that teased me, and clutched Sebastian's arm a little tighter, not drawing away when he covered my hand with his own, his movement nothing but proprietorial.

As I continued to look idly between the faces of the party guests, content for Sebastian to steer us in whatever direction he chose, I caught the gaze of Nicolas's uncle, and his features eased into a frown, a small line forming between his brows as he glanced at his nephew by my side.

I looked away. He didn't get to frown at the nephew showing me around when the nephew who'd brought me here apparently hadn't received good enough tuition on date night etiquette.

We walked out of the ballroom into a wide hallway not dissimilar to the one in Nicolas's home. Everything was hardwood or veined marble and reeked of class and culture.

"This is the salon." Sebastian indicated a double doorway to my left, and I glanced inside, taking in a slice of vintage French culture.

Huge, heavy velvet drapes hung ceiling to floor at numerous windows, and there were several small seating areas creating intimate spaces in the massive room. A grand piano took up deceptively little space in one corner, and there were candelabras on console tables and vases of brightly colored fresh flowers on other surfaces.

"It's beautiful." A little fussy and old-world for my tastes, maybe, but I could definitely appreciate the old money present here.

"A little old fashioned, perhaps." Sebastian spoke as if he'd read my mind and chuckled. "But if you like this style, there's definitely a room I want to show you."

He steered me toward a staircase, even grander and with more of a sweep than Nicolas's—and it made mine look like nothing more than a rickety ladder someone had propped against a wall. When we reached the foot of the stairs, I stopped.

"Where are we going?" I still had enough self-preservation not to be led to a strange man's bedroom.

He lifted his eyebrows suggestively. "Where would you like to go?"

As I hesitated further, he relaxed into a friendly grin.

"There's a sort of private gallery upstairs. Almost a museum." He shrugged. "I just thought it might interest you, that's all." A disappointed light entered his eyes. "We can go and check if Nic has finished reuniting with Aurelia instead, if you prefer?"

"No, I don't prefer." I tightened my hold on Sebastian and stepped onto the first tread. "I don't see any point in interrupting Nicolas and his friend."

And that much was true. Plus, the idea of facing the two of them, of potentially inserting myself where I really wasn't wanted, made my stomach lurch.

"If it's any consolation at all, I think Nic is crazy to let you wander around the party alone. I wouldn't let you leave my side if I'd brought you." Sebastian's voice was low, perhaps a little too close to my ear, but a frisson of pleasure skipped through me at the idea someone saw worth in me where Nicolas clearly didn't. Sebastian walked across a wide corridor toward a darkened room, and tugged me playfully toward him before flipping on the light. "I promise you're still within screaming distance of the party."

I relaxed at his teasing words. I was here as Nicolas's guest, this was his brother, their uncle had seen us leave the ballroom. It wasn't as if I'd been taken to the second location by a serial killer.

"Ta-da!" Sebastian flung his arm out with a flourish as we entered a room lined with shelves and filled with glass display cases. "The gallery," he added unnecessarily, and I smiled.

"Really?"

He chuckled. "Really, truly."

I let go of his arm as I wandered farther into the room, my attention caught by thick pottery urns that were cracked into several pieces. The designs were basic and faded.

"These look very old." My fingers hovered above the case, but I didn't even touch the glass.

"There's jewelry, too." Sebastian led me to another case filled with beaded necklaces and bracelets and intricately woven collars, peppered with much smaller beads.

"Wow. How did all of these things get to be here?" They honestly looked as though they belonged in a real museum.

Sebastian's lips quirked. "Father was quite a collector. He was a connoisseur, an antique expert... And also, I guess he was just a packrat.

Once he owned something, he couldn't bear to part with it."

Private collectors were a thing, and they definitely seemed to like to hoard rather than let everyone enjoy things in a public gallery, so it didn't seem so unreasonable to think Nicolas and Sebastian's father might have been one of those people.

However everything had arrived here, he was either very wealthy or had criminal connections. Probably both. A shiver rippled through me at that last thought. Maybe there was something wrong with this whole family.

This room certainly lent credence to the idea that I should find out what Nicolas was hiding, and after his continued mixed signals, it was in *my* best interest to not let this full month play out.

Except…except something in me wanted to stay. Like something was tugging me to stay… Or making it harder for me to want to leave, overriding all of my common sense. Shit. I'd *miss* him. Would *he* miss *me* after the month was over?

Horror expanded in my chest—I wanted to mean something to Nicolas, and that was stupid, so escape by any means was my only option before my ridiculous crush became a problem.

Because I did. I had a crush. And I couldn't let it continue. So I'd find out what I needed to know and pray it was enough to end the contract.

But I didn't ask Sebastian any more questions in case I received answers I didn't want to hear. He'd been right. We were still close enough to the ballroom that I could hear strains of music, and I relaxed a little as he beckoned me deeper into the room.

"Come and see this." He stood in front of a display case that was lit from within.

It held a silver comb that some aristocratic lady of Europe must have taken great delight in weaving into a fancy hairstyle. The comb shone under the lights, but it was so old that several of the teeth were missing.

"There's quite a legend attached to this piece," Sebastian said, watching me carefully as he spoke. "You believe in fairytales?" But his gaze remained serious, considering, waiting for my reply like it was important. "Want to hear one?"

I nodded, although there didn't seem to be too much anyone could say about such a fragile looking antique. It was probably an old family piece.

"Well… Once upon a time…" His lips quirked again, that expression of his now a familiar one, but his gaze remained serious.

I let myself lean forward a little, studying the comb as he talked.

"This is a very old hair decoration. You'll notice the inscription along the top." Sebastian brushed his fingers over the case, directly above the accessory, directing my attention to the piece. "*La beauté est eternelle*. It means *beauty is eternal*, and family legend says the comb was once enchanted by a witch to allow whoever wears it to remain beautiful regardless of their age." His voice lowered, taking on a seductive note. "Queens have killed for the chance to possess and wear this comb."

"Killed people?" I laughed lightly. "Good thing it's only a story."

His breath fanned across my neck, and I froze. He hadn't been this close to me when he started talking, and I hadn't heard him move. When he breathed again, the sound almost a low groan, a memory stirred, a sense of déjà-vu. Not like I'd been here with Sebastian before but that someone else—someone truly unwanted—had breathed against my neck.

I cleared my throat and straightened, attempting to step aside with purpose and dignity, even as my mind flashed through the possibilities. Could I still hear the music from the ballroom? Which route around the display cases and fragile items would take me to the door quickest?

But I didn't get a chance to even finish my thought or form a plan. As if he'd sensed my thoughts, Sebastian grasped my wrist and spun me to face him then backed me against the wall, his movements so fast, everything blurred. I struggled against him, but he took both of my wrists into his hand, his grasp bruisingly tight as my bones ground together. He leaned against me, aligning our bodies so there were no gaps between us as he dropped his head to the base of my throat.

"You smell amazing," he ground out as he rolled his hips against me. "How does Nic stand it? I was going to be nice, you know?" His tone became almost pleading. "Let him have you. But I don't know if I can." He clutched me tighter.

When I froze—everything inside me still, so much that I didn't even draw breath—Sebastian moved back far enough to meet my eyes.

His gaze glittered with menace and his mouth suddenly looked way too full. "I think you might be too good to pass up."

His voice was thick as he lowered his head toward my neck again, and I inhaled a deep breath because I needed to scream.

I had to scream, to do something. I couldn't just *freeze*.

"Let her go." *Nicolas.* His voice boomed across the museum room. "Step away, Sebastian."

Sebastian, still bent over my neck, sighed. "Oh, Nicolas. Always in the wrong place at the wrong time." But he shuffled backward, away from me, watching me the whole time, although I refused to meet his gaze. "You really need to pay more attention, though, Nic. And maybe I should act faster in future."

I looked at Nicolas, still so aware that Sebastian was much closer to me than I wanted, and Nicolas held out an arm toward me.

"Miss Boucher." He didn't smile. His expression didn't change at all, and I planned to walk toward him, dignity intact, head held high.

But I didn't. The moment I registered my name on his lips, I *ran* to him like I'd escaped the gates of hell, and I crashed against his body, shaking as he wrapped an arm around me to hold me closer to him.

For a moment, we just stood while I waited for my heartbeat to slow and my breathing to return to normal. Nicolas didn't do anything but remain slow and steady, firm and immovable for me to rest against, a protective arm around my back.

From somewhere behind me, Sebastian groaned quietly. "And the rear view is delectable, too."

Nicolas stiffened, each of his muscles tensing, and I glanced up at him.

"May we leave?" I was no longer in the mood for a party. I couldn't relax if I was trying to avoid Sebastian, and I felt weak and stupid.

Somewhere in the past few days, I'd lost myself. Where was the kickass bar owner from Baton Rouge who took shit from no one? But I didn't have too much time to ponder that before Nicolas nodded.

"Yes." He grated out the words. "We're leaving."

Chapter 14 - Nic

Leia jammed herself into the corner of the backseat, taking up as little room as possible, at least half an acre away from me. I left my hand resting in the gap between us, but she didn't take it. She didn't even look at me, even though I ached to touch her, the desperation of the anger that had run unchecked through me still unfamiliar and slow to recede.

I watched her, trying to only glance in her direction occasionally, but she couldn't see. Her forehead rested against the window, and when I caught sight of her reflection, her eyes were closed.

"Leia."

She stiffened. I so rarely used her name, preferring to allow her the distance she wanted, but now I didn't want any distance between us at all. I wanted her closer physically so I could reassure myself she was all right, and I didn't want her to start to reject me. I needed her trust.

Fucking Sebastian.

That bastard wanted everything that was mine. My parents, my throne, my fucking *mate.*

I turned my head away in case Leia glanced in my direction. Anger had caused an ache in my gums, and I needed to regain control of myself before I could talk to her as I wanted.

Damn Sebastian. I never lost control.

"Nicolas?" Her voice was hesitant.

"I'm sorry about Sebastian." I pushed the words past fangs that didn't want to retract, like my body still somehow sensed a threat to my mate.

My words seemed to open whatever dam had been holding her own words in.

"I don't even know what happened," she said. "I mean, what the hell was that? Why did Sebastian suddenly react like that? I was just... He just... I was looking at..." But she didn't finish, and I couldn't contain a dark chuckle.

"But you weren't in the ballroom." My heartrate picked up. She hadn't been safe. I'd almost been too late *again*.

"I… He's your *brother*." Her tone was flat, and she was right. It shouldn't have mattered.

In any normal fucking family, it wouldn't have mattered. My brother. The safest person she should have been with. But not the royal vampire family of Baton Rouge. Not any vampire family.

I clenched my first and rested it on my knee. "Sebastian has…issues."

"Then why was he there? Why did your uncle let me leave the room with him?"

I opened my mouth to reply, but Leia jumped back in.

"And don't even try to make this my fault for leaving the room again. Don't think I missed that the first time." She paused, and she'd clearly left the *you bastard* unsaid on the end of that last sentence.

I sighed. "No. No, you're right. I'm sorry."

"Where were you? Where did you go? Why do you keep taking me places and leaving me? The roof. The restaurant. The party." She listed my sins, and each one was like she scorched another mark on my heart.

I swallowed. "I was close by. Close enough to…help. I didn't intend for you to leave the restaurant or to leave the ballroom. And certainly not with…" Fuck. My gums ached again and I'd just regained control. "With Sebastian."

"But what the hell happened to your brother?" When she looked at me, barely contained fury shone in her eyes. "Did you see him? His eyes were cold and angry and kind of dead-looking, and his mouth was weird. Like he'd suddenly grown a bunch more teeth in there. I couldn't work out if he wanted to kill me or eat me. He was strong, too. And fast."

She shuddered, her fear and revulsion visible.

Fuck. She'd seen too much. She was skirting too close to the truth now. I sighed again, strategically this time, the sigh of a long-suffering sibling tired of his brother's antics.

"I'm sorry." I could keep apologizing and it would never be enough. "He really does have his problems." That much was true. My parents had spoiled their made children, treating them as well as they treated me, and they'd made Sebastian entitled. "He will never come near you again."

She lifted an eyebrow. "*Never* is a pretty big promise, Nicolas."

Then she narrowed her eyes and angled her body toward me, and I got ready to sigh again. Or apologize. This could go either way. None of this conversation was turning out well, and I didn't think I'd ever sighed as much in my life.

"Speaking of never seeing him again, weird question, but...have I ever seen him before?" She touched her temple and grimaced like something had hurt her.

"No." I gripped the handle on the door, almost afraid to ask, and fucking hell, I was never afraid.

Only this ridiculous human affected me like that. *Ridiculous human...* Who the hell was I kidding? Her power over me and my kind was immense.

"Why?" I forced myself to ask.

"Because..." She looked uncertain, one corner of her mouth tugging on her cheek. "I mean, I had the weirdest sense of déjà-vu when he was up against me. Breathing on my neck, telling me I smelled nice... Shit." She waved a hand. "That's just any drunk guy looking to get some, right? But it felt... I don't know. Familiar? Recent?"

I closed my eyes briefly. Dammit. My compulsion wouldn't hold much longer, not if her memories were already struggling to resurface. I'd deliberately only used light compulsion—enough to relax her and push bad memories to the very back of her mind, not take them away completely—but this was a fast recovery.

She'd had that amethyst pendant on, so maybe it was that acting against my abilities, or perhaps it was her ancestry that had conflicted the results.

She came from a long line of strong women. More than strong. Gifted, and Leia was the result of all that powerful Louisiana blood. A gift from the ages just for me.

That she was already asking questions meant only one thing—I'd have to tell her who I was. *What* I was. But I looked at her, taking in her pale face, her teeth nibbling her lower lip, the too-wide eyes with purple marks beneath, and shook my head slightly.

Not now.

She was too fragile now.

We arrived home, my hand still uselessly on the seat between us, and Jenkins opened her door first. She almost sprinted toward the open front door, stopping only briefly to greet Baldwin before barreling through, and I jogged to catch up to her.

"Leia." I used her name again as I reached for her, but she flinched away.

"I think I just need to be alone." She drew in on herself, becoming smaller even as I watched.

"But I can help," I said, even though I called bullshit on myself. I had no right to tell her I could help when I didn't know if I could do anything at all. But I wanted her near me. She kept wandering away, and that clearly wasn't safe.

"No." Her eyes blazed with sudden fire. "No, Nicolas, you *can't* help. I don't trust you to keep me safe. I don't want you near me."

She took a step towards the stairs like she was edging to safety, and the movement lit a spark of my own anger.

"Where are you going?" My words came out tight and controlled.

"To my room." She was defiant, still edging away. "To be alone, like I said."

"Your room in *my* house, during *my* month." I spat out the words, awareness at my own stupidity already echoing through my thoughts.

My house? My month? Who the hell had I become? My father?

"You're safer with me." I tried to gentle my voice, but it still came out as a command.

She barked out a sudden laugh. "That's rich. I was with you this evening if I recall—"

"You *left*," I interjected, my voice flat. "You left with Sebastian and endangered yourself."

Leia's skirts rustled as she climbed several steps, putting herself above me before she turned around. Fuck, she was beautiful when she was angry. Fire and fury blazed from her, and I basked in it even as I railed against it, wanting her back under my control.

"I wasn't safe at the home of your family, or with your brother, and I no longer feel safe here. Connect the dots, Dupont. You haven't kept me safe. You can't keep me safe. I'd be safer if I left. Maybe you're the boogeyman, too."

Her use of my last name was a slap in the face, and I stepped closer to the stairs, grabbing hold of the end of the winding bannister where it finished in a tight spiral, my knuckles whitening, the wood threatening to crack under the force of my grip.

My chest heaved with the injustice of Leia running from me based on my brother's actions.

"I would never scare you like Sebastian did." Then I checked myself and lowered my voice. Shouting at her wasn't the best way to convince her of the sincerity of my words. "Why would you think me capable of that?"

"Because you're brothers. You share blood," she said, and then she whirled away, flouncing up the stairs.

On the sharing blood thing, she was very wrong indeed. I would never share the same blood as Sebastian, and he would most certainly not share *anything* that was mine.

I prowled through the first floor of my home, then the basement, irritable and aware of Leia's presence, lurking like a shadow in the east wing. The same shadow lurked in my head, nudging me into a constant state of arousal and desire. Just knowing she was close by made me want her, even as I wanted to comfort her and make her feel safe. I had a desire to protect her as much as fuck her. It burned like a fierce need in my chest.

When the need grew too much, I stormed up the stairs, hesitating outside the doors to the east wing. She'd closed them, mirroring the doors of the west wing—a clear indication that I wasn't welcome in her space.

I whirled away and unlocked the doors to the west wing, slamming them for the sheer theater of ensuring Leia knew I'd also rejected her this evening. I hoped she cared.

Except. Fuck. No. I didn't care if she cared at all. I didn't need her to *want* me. Just to accept me willingly. I didn't care how she fucking *felt*. I didn't feel anything at all.

Apart from anger.

I shoved the rejection down and ignored it.

I walked toward my room then stopped, resting my hand on the doorhandle of the first door I came across. I kept this room closed. I never looked inside. This room had been reserved for decades for my bride.

But now I flung the door open and strode inside, my chest heaving with each deep inhale as I sought an outlet for my building rage. I had no bride.

I had no fucking bride. No queen. No way to secure my rule. And it seemed like I was blowing my one chance.

I tore through the room, pushing furniture over and ripping the white drapes on the four-poster bed. This was a room for my virgin, and she wouldn't even let me near her. She'd closed me out.

I whirled around the space like a tornado, tearing my nails down antique wood, releasing feathers from the pillows, and shredding soft furnishings. By the time I stood by the door, my chest still heaving, nothing in the room was usable anymore.

But it didn't matter.

She didn't fucking want me.

Shit. What was wrong with me?

I left my bride's room and…fuck. I needed a drink. I made my way to my… I laughed. My *wine cellar*. Except it wasn't wine. It was all neatly bagged and organized according to vintage, though.

My blood room was quiet with only the unrelenting hum of the refrigerators, and I immediately missed Leia. I felt the lack of her just as acutely as I ever felt her presence.

I grabbed and warmed a pouch of blood, but my stomach soured at the idea of drinking it, swallowing the too-thick, slightly curdled liquid that had already lost most of its vitality.

Maybe these would never satisfy me again. Not now I was so aware of the blood thrumming through Leia's body.

My blood.

I wanted her to come to me willingly, but maybe she never would. And that made this world unsafe for her. I rested my head back against my chair and stretched my legs out ahead of me, crossing them at the ankles.

It didn't need to be this difficult. And it wouldn't be if I just bit her. I *could* actually just bite her. I tilted my head as I mused on that. I wouldn't be able to continue as king if I forfeited her willing participation, but Leia would be safe from those looking to challenge me.

And she'd be mine.

Chapter 15 - Leia

I woke cranky, my throat sore, tangled in my sheets. I'd clearly had a restless night, and not for a good reason. Despite myself, my traitorous thoughts pictured Nicolas Dupont tangled in the sheets with me, his limbs heavy as they rested over mine, pinning me to the bed with lazy possessiveness.

I shook my head then rolled over and screamed into my pillow. That infuriating man. He didn't belong in my head, dangerously close to my fantasies.

But the memory of the way he'd touched me...the way my body had responded to him and how my name sounded spilling from his lips as he encouraged me higher. It had all been a very dazzling spell.

I lifted my head to inhale to scream again, but a soft knock at the door stopped me.

"Miss Boucher?" Nicolas's voice was soft this morning. Not quite contrite but more hesitant than I was used to.

And I was back to being *Miss Boucher.* Of course. But that was for the best. I needed out of this ridiculous contract. If all Dupont parties ended in me being scared out of my mind, a month was going to be a very long time.

But I still wanted my house. And I wanted my bar. And I was fucking well going to get them.

I huffed and flopped on my back.

"Miss Boucher?" His voice came again, slightly louder this time.

"I'm sick. I just need to rest." My voice was sleep swollen and croaky enough to throw weight behind my claim, but I sensed him hesitate before he spoke again.

"I need to go to La Pet—" He broke off. "The casino," he said, like he couldn't force out the full name any more than I wanted to hear those words. Too many memories of his skillful fingers came flooding back. He hesitated again like he expected a reply before his next words came more muffled, like he'd rested his forehead against the door between us. "I'll have someone check on you."

For the next few moments, I just waited in silence, barely even breathing, like he might hear my thoughts if he was still standing too close. And outside my bedroom door was definitely too close when all of my thoughts were about to consist of how to sneak places I wasn't meant to go in his house.

After the treasures I'd seen last night, coupled with the behavior of his brother, it was clear that the Duponts were obviously rich and without morals, which suggested some degree of criminality. And when I linked that with the stylists strange talk about rules, the coded language they seemed to use...was I in some sort of mafia territory? Organized crime in Baton Rouge? It didn't seem possible, yet here I was. Considering it.

Maybe even starting to believe it.

After all, what more perfect place to mastermind a criminal enterprise from than a casino full of undesirables? And a notorious one…where even the name conjured hot memories.

I groaned. I needed to get my head out of the gutter. And I needed to find something against Nicolas Dupont that would have him forgetting our contract or tearing it up or setting it on fire just to be rid of me.

And that evidence was most likely in his locked wing.

So that was where I needed to go.

I tugged the comforter over myself and made myself into a human cinnamon roll. I'd wait until I knew Nicolas had really gone and things had quieted down.

There was another small knock at the door, and Emma appeared with a tray of food. "The master said for me to bring your breakfast to you this morning. How are you feeling now?" Her voice was quiet, sympathetic, and I withheld a sob that threatened to work its way up my throat. Pity always undid me. "Chef sent some more beignets and one of his special hot chocolates."

I murmured a noise that she could interpret any way she wanted and prayed for the low growl of my stomach not to betray me. I couldn't eat the food. I needed them to think I was truly sick.

Emma sighed a little and slipped from the room, and the tray was still exactly where she'd left it when Jason appeared a short while later.

"How are you feeling?" Even he kept his voice low, and I longed to be deserving of the care and respect these people showed to someone they thought was sick. "Can I get you anything?"

Hmm. That was a question I hadn't expected from Nicolas's bodyguard. But I needed him to leave the house so I could ensure he wasn't hanging around outside my door, still on his ridiculous guard duty. Only possibly not so ridiculous today because he really needed to be on guard against my behavior rather than doing the usual thing of protecting me.

"My robe," I croaked out. "It's at my house. I always wear it when I'm sick."

A half-smile crossed Jason's face. "Has Nic not provided you with a robe? Sometimes, I think he knows nothing about women."

I glanced toward the bathroom and thought guiltily of the hotel-quality robe hanging on the hook behind the door. "My robe was my mother's." That much was true. It was old and threadbare but wearing it still brought comfort. I was only telling half a lie. "Can you get it?"

Conflict marred his features. "I shouldn't leave you alone."

I forced a cough and rolled myself deeper before turning what I knew was my most practiced pitiful gaze on him. It always worked on Harry, anyway. "Please?"

Jason watched me for a while longer, his eyes narrowed, and I saw the exact moment he relented. "All right." He cleared his throat. "Just don't get out of bed."

I made another noncommittal noise, stopping short of actually lying, and closed my eyes like I might sleep. "Thank you, Jason," I whispered just before the bedroom door clicked shut. Then a tear escaped a corner of my eyes because I'd probably just fucked up that fledgling friendship.

I waited a few minutes, then stood at the window, peering from behind the drape as I held it aside just the smallest fraction. Jason set off down the driveway, and I released a sigh of relief. He shouldn't be back for at least an hour. More if he got caught in traffic.

I wriggled into the hoodie I'd brought with me and a pair of my old jeans, and I quietly opened the bedroom door and crept down the hallway, the thick carpet cushioning my footfalls. I reached my double doors and had a clear view of the west wing double doors as they stood open. *Score*! I hadn't planned much beyond brute strength or an attempt at lockpicking, but open doors was like fate herself had rolled out the welcome mat.

I crept out of my doors as a flash of movement from Nicolas's wing caught my eyes, and I ducked back against the wall, hardly daring breathe as Mrs. Ames backed out of the corridor I'd been about to enter. She was singing loudly and off-key, the noise competing with the low hum of the vacuum cleaner.

She pulled the door closed and reached in her pocket like she was looking for keys but came up empty. Shaking her head, she powered off the vacuum and walked away, and I seized my chance, slipping into the west wing and checking I'd be able to get out even if she locked the door. I clicked it closed behind me, anyway, hoping she'd think someone else had already secured it in her absence.

I hadn't been prepared for the dark. No light filtered from the various rooms because all of the doors along the hallway were closed, and any windows that might have allowed the daylight in were covered. It was like I'd stepped into a grave, and a shiver washed over my skin.

I opened the first door I came to and switched on the light, then stifled a gasp. A beautiful room had been destroyed. It looked like a cross between a werewolf and a Tasmanian devil had whirled through, all claws and sharp teeth, shredding and tearing apart. Claw marks raked down the posts of a bed that must have been spectacular, but now the canopy was shredded, and feathers from the half-empty pillows covered the room like a layer of snow. There was beauty in the ruin now it was peaceful, but the level of violence that had taken place here gripped my chest in an icy fist, and I struggled to draw my next full breath.

Back out in the corridor, I allowed the quiet and darkness to blanket me with calm, wrapping myself in those shadows as I crept to the next closed door. Once open, it revealed a room similar to the one where Sebastian had been on the verge of attacking me at the party. I swallowed against a rush of bile and glanced between the glass display cases. I had no interest in whatever artifacts Nicolas was hoarding.

I'd originally wondered if their crime empire was built on drugs, but stolen art and antiques was looking far more likely, however that worked. Still, crime was crime, and I had to be able to find *something* to blackmail Nicolas into letting me out of our contract. I was about to become the biggest pain in his ass he'd ever known.

I threw one last glance around the room, already closing the door, but then I stopped. Paintings. So many paintings lined the walls, and a familiar gaze blazed from all of them. Against my will, my feet carried me into the room, and I walked along the line of paintings, taking in the thick brushstrokes of bold oils and the gloomy color palette of years gone by. So many historical periods…

And Nicolas in all of them.

I choked back a laugh, almost unable to imagine Nicolas Dupont being *this* much into cosplay that he'd commission portraits of himself in historical dress. Such a strange thing to collect. But as follies went, it was possibly forgivable. Even if I did give them a little more side-eye.

As I moved forward in time—the paintings becoming more realistic, losing that strange round-eyed quality of historical portraits—to modern day now, with Nicolas in his usual black-on-black suit—he became increasingly handsome. Even immortalized in paint, there was something hypnotic about him, and every single painter had captured whatever quality it was about Nicolas that made him so hard to resist.

Because I did want to resist him.

But escape seemed a more likely bet.

I shuddered at the word *bet* in relation to Nicolas Dupont. *The house always wins.* Those were his words, I knew that much. I needed to win this time. I needed to get away unscathed and with my future intact.

I took one last, long look at the line of paintings, committing this Nicolas, the one with the half-smile that said he already knew most of my secrets, to memory. Then I left the room and closed the door, relief swallowing me that the corridor was still quiet, still calm. I needed to find something fast, though. I had to be back in bed before Jason returned with Mom's robe.

I walked quickly to the next door. Stealth was almost guaranteed on these floors, and I couldn't afford to waste time tiptoeing or being distracted by ruined rooms or odd portraits. I rested my hand on the next door I came to, about to push it open when I stopped and pressed my ear to the door.

Something inside the room was humming steadily. Maybe I'd seen too many true crime documentaries, but the first thought in my head was freezers. Or just a giant walk-in like at an slaughterhouse, with hooks in the ceiling and dead bodies just hanging around the place…chilling.

I snorted nervous amusement and listened again. The hum was constant. Definitely a fan or something similar, and unlikely to be a computer. But had I really made the leap from art thief to serial killer between the last room and this one?

I leaned my forehead against the door, almost tempted to return to my room. I couldn't do anything from there, though. Get right back into bed? Pack and leave? Neither of those seemed like viable alternatives. I couldn't leave before getting the contract cancelled, and I couldn't stay in the home of a potential mass murderer.

My mind whirled with too many questions I couldn't answer from the hallway, so I took a deep breath then pushed the door open.

Wall-to-wall refrigerators. *What the fuck?* I stood in the doorway like I'd walked into a freezer after all—completely frozen.

I swallowed, but it was painful and noisy as I forced it around the lump in my throat. The refrigerators were stainless steel and industrial looking, but definitely more busy restaurant than local morgue. There was a lab table in the middle of the room and a... I looked closer. Weird—a baby bottle warmer sat on the table, although I was pretty sure these fridges didn't contain formula.

No one had mentioned a baby, and they were pretty difficult to keep quiet.

"Curiouser and curiouser," I murmured as I walked to the first fridge.

A glass cabinet stood against the wall behind me, rows of test tubes visible behind the glass doors at the top, but I ignored those. I wanted to know what all of these fridges held. Art thief was still in the running for Nicolas's crimes, but serial killer was looking a little more likely.

Until I opened the first fridge. And *holy hell.*

More little blood-filled baggies than would ever be

collected at a local blood drive. And it was definitely blood because it was labelled by blood type and other identifying details such as sex and age of donor.

Like…*what. The. Hell?*

I opened the next fridge, the door heavy as it swung open, a sense of dread already in the pit of my stomach and climbing higher, squeezing my breath out of me.

More baggies of blood, but a different blood type. And the third fridge was the same again. Same jewel red, different vintage. But why the hell would Nicolas Dupont keep blood on hand like he was amassing a collection of fine wine?

I stood back and looked at all three of the fridges, doors hanging open, the wire shelves stacked with orderly trays of blood bags. Then I remembered the cabinet with the test tubes. There were doors I couldn't see through, too, so I turned to investigate further—and almost walked straight into Nicolas.

He stood, arms folded, shirt sleeves rolled up his forearms in a way that made me want to lick his skin. Or bite him and leave my mark. Where the hell was his jacket?

Stupid thoughts filled my head as I tried not to give in to the kind of panic that would freeze me and make me unable to act. Shit. *Fucking* shit. I was in the one place I wasn't supposed to be, with a possible *serial killer*. Alarm and also shame crowded my thoughts, and I had to focus to breathe.

But I shook my head, trying to free myself from emotions that could paralyze me. I was here, Nicolas had found me, and it wasn't ideal, but… I could be a grown-up about this. I skimmed my gaze up his body from his feet, taking my time before I dared meet his eyes. I already knew they'd be angry.

"Hello." My voice came out as a squeak. He had the same dead expression I'd seen on Sebastian last night, and the edge of his pupils seemed to glow red as he looked past me at the open refrigerator doors.

For the first time, true ice-cold fear filled me in Nicolas's presence. He'd always been vaguely intimidating, keeping me kind of off balance, but I'd managed to convince myself I was safe with him. That he was honorable. But now, in this room, I doubted all my instincts.

Why had I ever believed that?

I backed away from him, my breath pushing from my body in spurts. My eyes widened until they were almost painful, but I didn't dare look away and I didn't dare blink.

Nicolas matched me step for step, a slow, easy predator, following me until my ass hit a wall.

I'd cornered myself.

Chapter 16 - Nic

My head pounded like it might explode, and my gums ached as my fangs pressed against them, threatening to rip through. I couldn't even speak to Leia to express my rage—I just had to stand there, watching her, considering all the words I wanted to say.

Her eyes widened, her fear obvious. I could smell it, and fuck...it aroused me. My cock pressed against my pants as my fangs pressed against my gums, and I groaned at the pressure. I closed my eyes briefly, and when I opened them again, Leia still looked terrified, an expression I hadn't seen on her face the whole time we'd been together. Maybe not even with Sebastian.

I forced myself to draw a calming breath. Then another.

"This is *my* private space," I ground out.

She nodded, the movement quick and bird-like. "Yes."

The word came out on a breath, and I clenched my fists, angry with her for being scared of me, furious at myself for making her that way.

"You shouldn't have come here."

She shook her head this time. "No. No, I... I..."

I glanced again at the open fridges behind her. Fuck. She could have ruined everything by coming in here and opening those. She'd have questions now. Too many.

How the *fucking hell* would I answer her questions? Damn Sebastian. He set all of this shit in motion.

I leaned toward Leia, and the scent of fear grew stronger. At the last moment, I slammed the fridge door closest to us, and she flinched, her knees buckling as she slumped harder against the wall. I whirled away and slammed the remaining doors, releasing her from the wall at the same time.

"Sit down." My words were a growl, and she flinched again but bolted toward the open door instead of the low sofa I'd pointed at.

"Leia." I reached for her and hauled her back as I snapped her name, and she squealed as my arms wrapped around her. "I said to *sit*. Not run away. You *will not run away from me*."

I boomed the last words, the volume driven by a sudden spike of dread.

She was running. I was the monster I'd never wanted to be to her. And I needed her, craved the power only she could bring me. But need had started giving way to want, and a little spark of reliance glowed in my chest. I wanted to be around her and for her to want to be with me.

I sat next to her, and she squashed herself to one end of the couch, taking up half as much room as she probably needed to be comfortable.

"I need you to stay so I can explain," I said, trying to make my voice reasonable. Gentle, even.

I reached for her but retracted my hand when she shifted away, not even meeting my gaze.

"Don't touch me," she spat, and I almost smiled at the fire that still blazed in her despite any fear or uncertainty this room had caused.

"What are you doing in my private wing?" Okay. That was good. I'd asked a reasonable question in a reasonable tone of voice. Ten reasonable points to me.

I glanced at her, but her gaze darted to the door, and her posture was tense like she was spring-loaded and might take off running at any point. I didn't want to chase her through the house, but I was faster than her, and I *would* catch her.

I sighed. That kind of behavior would scare her and raise even more questions for me to answer.

"Please stay," I murmured. "Please don't run away. I know you have questions, so ask them and I'll tell you what you want to know."

"Oh my God." She closed her eyes and rocked a little, and it didn't even look like she was talking to me. "Oh my God." She pinched the inside of her arm. "Wake up," she murmured. "Fucking wake up."

I waited, just watching her. My breathing calmed even as her breaths increased, and I focused on regaining my control. I could handle this. It was a curve ball, but I could handle it.

Finally, she looked at me. "Not a dream." Her voice was flat, expressionless, and her eyes were without the usual light.

"Not a dream." I shook my head as sadness wound through my thoughts. "Where's Jason?"

Leia's eyes narrowed. "Don't even try to make this his fault. I assume he's not the one with a wall full of the world's oldest selfies and fridges filled with more blood than the local blood bank."

I shrugged. "I couldn't presume to comment on Jason's taste in art or the contents of his fridge."

"*Nicolas.*"

I sighed. "What are your questions?" It was better to let her lead than risk saying too much.

The sound she made was somewhere between a frustrated huff and a strangled chuckle as she threw her arms up and we both bounced a little on the cushions of the loveseat. "Just…" She looked around. "All of it. Why? What *is this*?"

I took a breath to form an answer, but she wasn't finished.

"*All* the damn questions, actually. Who, what, how, where, when, *why*? Are…are you a criminal? A serial killer? What the hell was with that bedroom that someone had torn to shreds? Why do you have a treasure room with freaky pictures of you dressed up? And for the love of all that's holy, why do you have fridges and fridges of blood? Trophies?"

When she finished, a mixture of confusion and pain blazed in her eyes, but the pain gave me hope. I could work with hurt. It would have been harder if she felt nothing.

Hurt feelings could be soothed. They could be turned.

In my experience, hurt feelings led to make up sex, and I'd be happy to get halfway back to that. *Fucking Sebastian.* All of this shit was still his fault. If he hadn't inserted himself into my business, I might have claimed Leia last night.

That had been my plan after finding her so willing in the car, anyway. I should have just done it. I should have had Jenkins just turn the car around and take us home. My time would have been so much better spent between my sheets, over Leia, inside her, my cock moving to the same rhythm as her blood spilling down my throat.

I shifted, adjusting my pants discreetly.

"Well?" She raised an eyebrow.

"Once upon a time…" I deadpanned, and she flinched.

"Do all Dupont men begin stories that way?" She moved farther away, stealing a hair's breadth of space to put more distance between us.

Fucking Sebastian.

I tried again, spreading my arms, my palms upturned, to show I had nothing to hide. This still needed to work. Maybe I could keep Leia and secure my throne, or just keep Leia safe. I had to try *something*, anyway. She was in too much danger now that I'd revealed her to our society. But it wasn't exactly the easiest story to tell a human, and I'd expected to have more time.

"I'm very old," I started. "Impossibly old. I was born in France, and those portraits are me. Truly me. Not in period dress. Not random flights of fancy. Me. Accurate. Of my time, in historical context. Do you understand?"

She nodded, but the bewildered edge didn't leave her expression.

"My father was a king among my people. He's still thought of that way. But there was a battle between clans, and my family had to flee France. We travelled to the new world to start afresh—like every immigrant before us and since, I guess." I shrugged, because the reason we'd travelled to the land of the free was no different than anyone else who'd stepped foot on America's shores. "Like many, we began our journey in Virginia, but the colony was small, and we quickly moved on because my family fares better in isolation or in a large crowd where few people are truly noticed and fewer still are missed. We spent some time in Roanoke, but that went badly." I almost chuckled at some of the older memories. *Badly* was an understatement.

Fucking Sebastian.

"When the French claimed Louisiana, it seemed like the perfect solution. We could be back among our people, some of our old ways."

Leia wasn't saying anything or registering much awareness, so I reached for her hand. Her skin was like ice beneath my fingers, but when she didn't immediately pull away, I started stroking my thumb over her, reflexively trying to encourage warmth back into her.

"We were familiar with the language and the customs, and despite the jungle-like conditions and the sharp-toothed, reptilian inhabitants, we could hold our own. Father saw potential here for his new kingdom, and he was right. Louisiana has been home for many years, the constant change and evolution providing the camouflage we needed to blend in."

She looked at me then, her gaze seeming to focus. "You've been here many years?"

I nodded, taking comfort in entangling our fingers together as I told my story. "I've known your maternal line for longer than I can remember, from when they first came to Baton Rouge and settled here. I've protected your ancestors, commiserated their losses, celebrated their wins over the years. The women of your family have always been strong, each powerful in their own way. Like you."

Her eyes widened a little, but she clenched her jaw and tipped her chin up a little. "Did you know my mother?"

A smile captured my lips as I remembered Camille. I'd always admired her and regretted the way Jean treated her with so much casual disrespect, but I could never have imagined she would leave me a gift such as Leia. I hadn't even thought of that all the times I extended Jean's tab and granted him more and more outlandish items as collateral against his debt.

"Yes. Camille was…" How could I sum Leia's mother up for her? "On the one hand, she was fae-like and hard to capture, but she had an inner strength and light that no one could dim. Your father lived and breathed for her."

I shook my head as I recalled their early marriage and matched that up with Jean's later descent into the bottom of the nearest bottle of bourbon.

"And then she died." Leia's eyes welled with tears, and one slid from the outer corner of her eye.

I caught it on the pad of my thumb.

"And then she died," I agreed sadly, and guilt washed over me because I hadn't been there. "I… I lost touch with your mother because my own father was dying and I needed to maintain his rule while he couldn't. I didn't pay as much attention as I should have. I wasn't there."

Leia folded in on herself, her hands over her face, her shoulders shaking, and I waited a moment before I drew her against my chest, unsure of my welcome, unsure if this crossed the boundaries I'd set for myself.

My move from tolerating this human to actively comforting her had been a big step. And it was one that could potentially earn me a swift elbow to the balls after all she'd seen in my personal wing of the house.

Chapter 17 - Leia

Too many thoughts tumbled through my head, and no matter how I tried to arrange them, they were an impossible jigsaw puzzle. Nothing made sense. Nicolas was impossibly old? Old? What the hell? The guy in front of me wasn't *old*.

But the comments about Mom. About Dad. Was that just cruelty? Another game from the man who'd contracted to own me for one month?

I'd faked being sick earlier, but I was truly sick now. Sick and completely exhausted.

But I couldn't walk away. I couldn't fucking walk away, no matter how much I longed to.

Nicolas seemed to know just which button to press, and the Mom button was a doozy. Whether he was full of shit about whatever fucking immortality and knowing her or not, she was the reason I was even here.

I needed to make her proud. And that reminder of her was enough to keep me in this house as long as I needed to be here to achieve all of my goals.

My head was heavy, my eyes felt full, and my face ached. Nicolas wiped another tear from my cheek, the gesture so tender my heart cramped at all that could have been if we hadn't gone to that party.

He watched me, an unusual uncertainty in his gaze like he was laying everything on the line, like maybe this wasn't something he did, and that gave me confidence.

"I asked a bunch of questions."

He nodded. "You did." His mouth didn't even twitch. This was a serious conversation with no high-handed amusement.

"But you didn't answer any. You only introduced more."

His expression didn't change. He merely watched me like he was waiting for the next words out of my mouth. And I was waiting for a prompt.

Something that would let me know it was okay to ask the things I needed to know.

Even pondering the questions in my head made me question my sanity, but currently one of us was insane…and I called dibs on being the one who… Hell. I didn't even know what I wanted.

"One of us is crazy," I moaned as I drew away from him, back to my safe space, almost on a cushion just for myself. He was so big and took up so much room. And he might have been magnetic. I wanted to touch him, for him to touch me. When he held me, he soothed me. Despite everything.

"How so?" His question took me by surprise.

"Really? We're having this whole conversation about you being impossibly old in a room filled with blood bags and one of us *isn't* crazy?"

The amused twist to his lips returned, but he inclined his head in acknowledgement or concession. "Put that way…"

"So?" I lifted my chin toward him, prompting him to answer the question I hadn't asked, the one I didn't even want to *think*.

"So?" His voice was soft, a little of the deadly predator I'd come to recognize in him evident.

I released a long slow sigh, a hiss of air as I finally deflated and let go of any confidence or certainty I was holding onto in this situation. Feeling as crazy as I'd joked about being, I asked, "So, Nicolas Dupont, the impossibly long-lived man…what are you?"

His eyes flickered like he was surprised I'd put the question into words, that it was finally free in the space between us. Then he held my hands, his grip soft but still strong.

I looked into his eyes, and they took on a red hue, almost glowing. For a moment, he looked like Sebastian, but I couldn't draw away. Something inside me wanted to press closer.

"*Vampire*," he whispered.

"For fuck's sake," I blurted as I yanked my hands from him and whirled away to stand a short distance from him. "You could at least take me seriously."

But my stomach clenched and my legs trembled as I squeezed my eyes closed. *Vampire.* The word echoed in my mind, and the truth of it resonated deep inside me, even though the logical part of me was screaming about how absolutely *insane* that was.

I shook my head. "You can't be. Vampires are just stories. Fairytales. Things we talk about to frighten our children and our women into behaving."

"Do I frighten you?" Nicolas's voice was no more than a seductive rumble behind me as his chest pressed against my back and his warmth seeped into me.

A strangled sound escaped my throat at his proximity. "If you are what you say you are, you should."

His hand drifted down my upper arm, and heat flared through me before coming to settle between my legs. He drew a breath.

"Jesus Christ," he groaned. "You're aroused."

"Ha!" I spun around and jabbed my finger in his chest. "You're not a vampire. How did you say *Jesus Christ?*"

He clutched a hand over his heart and staggered before standing straight again and grinning, the effect maddening in its attractiveness. "Because holy hell, Leia, churches, crosses, and religious words don't affect me."

"Okay." I looked around the room. "Okay then." My tone turned challenging. "Well, there's no way a fucking *vampire* would arouse me."

His grin intensified, and his voice grew soft again as he stepped closer and looked down at me. "Well, I *am* very sexy, Miss Boucher."

I took a breath and stepped back, looking away from the gray eyes I suddenly wanted to be whirled away in. They were turbulent today, like a storm was coming, and I shivered. "But I've seen you eat."

He nodded. "Yes."

I laughed. "Well, vampires don't do that."

He examined his nails for a moment then glanced at me. "Really? All vampires or just the sparkly ones?"

I folded my arms and tapped my foot. "All the vampires I know."

His gaze darkened. "Do you know many vampires?"

I huffed out a groan. "You're making me as crazy as you are. Didn't you hear me when I said vampires are fairytales? They're not *real*."

Nicolas moved so fast he was a blur in front of me as he carried me backward until I bumped against the wall. His arm was wrapped around me, cushioning the blow, but I gasped at the unexpected impact.

"Vampires aren't fairytales, Miss Boucher," he growled, low and menacing. "We're nightmares."

As I watched him, his cheekbones sharpened, and the dull red color I'd noticed in his eyes before returned but glowed like the ruby gems I'd worn on last night's necklace, and fangs descended from his gums.

My heartrate kicked up until I thought my heart might explode right out of my chest, splattering both of us with blood, gore, and the remnants of my lifeforce. My ribs squeezed and I tried to draw breath, but it stuck.

I closed my eyes, needing space, needing Nicolas to back away from me, but he didn't. He leaned closer until the ends of his hair grazed my cheek and those impossible fangs grazed my neck.

"Leia." My name was almost a groan of pain as he held himself still. His warm breath skimmed my skin, and I stayed perfectly still, waiting.

I felt each inhale in the way his chest broadened and the soft sounds he made so close to my ear, and desire uncoiled inside me, lazy and filled with memories of the way he'd already touched me.

He held perfectly still for just a moment longer before his tongue swiped delicately up my neck, and I shivered. "You tempt me." Then he pressed soft, open-mouthed kisses along my jaw. "Do I tempt you?"

I breathed out a quiet moan of protest. I didn't want to be tempted. He had fangs. He was a *vampire*. He shouldn't even have existed outside folklore. And he'd had his fingers inside me. I'd enjoyed his kisses. Craved more.

He drew away from me, his eyes a soft dark gray, facial features no longer as harsh, fangs retracted. "Do you believe me now?"

I nodded. The dangerous air that clung to him made sense now. My stomach roiled as he turned from me and walked away.

Nicolas Dupont, casino owner.

My owner for one calendar month.

Vampire.

It didn't make sense. And maybe we really were both crazy, standing in a room of blood, believing in creatures of the night.

I walked shakily back to the loveseat, even though I wanted nothing more than to stride confidently out of the door. But fear or lust had weakened me—and I didn't want to examine those choices too closely because I didn't feel good about either of them.

Nicolas approached the fridges, opened them all back up, and stood for a moment like he was considering the contents. Then he shut two of the doors and reached into the third to extract one of the bags. He put it in the bottle warmer and grabbed a mug from the cabinet I'd been about to explore when he walked into the room.

The mug had a cartoon picture of a Venus flytrap on the front, but the plant had eyes and two huge fangs. *I want to suck your blood* was written in a dripping red font underneath the plant, and Nicolas laughed when he saw where I was looking.

His cheeks reddened, like this moment—out of all the things I'd just seen and he'd just said—embarrassed him. He lifted the mug in my direction. "This is an ironic gift from my sister because I'm the only one of us who doesn't take blood directly from the vein."

He poured his warmed blood into the mug, and a slightly stale coppery smell filled the air. When he took a sip, he grimaced, and I watched him as I pondered his words.

"You have a sister?" I blurted the question.

He laughed, the sound of genuine amusement sudden and unexpected. "*That's* what you took from what I just said?"

I wrapped my arms around myself, warding off a chill, and nodded. "I mean, I have other questions, but I'm still digesting."

He laughed again before he took another sip from his mug. "Fair. Yes, I have brothers and sisters. Not sure how many. Every now and again, a new one pops up from nowhere. They're all made. But I was born to my parents."

He said that like it was an important distinction, so I nodded.

"Was she at the party?" I couldn't help the shudder that ran through me as I thought of the party, and Nicolas's eyes tightened as he noticed it.

He shook his head. "No. I don't see many of my brothers and sisters very often. Sebastian is only here for the—" He broke off and looked into his mug like he'd said too much.

It was the first time I'd seen Nicolas Dupont look truly uncertain, and that vulnerability looked good on him.

"For the what?" I must have been in shock. I was currently sitting in a vampire's lair, and we were having an actual conversation. But I couldn't escape the feeling he was so much more than a vampire.

Something much more important.

He cleared his throat as he swirled his mug, the same movement I frequently made with my coffee, or that killer hot chocolate I occasionally allowed myself to buy from the boutique coffee shop tucked away from the tourist areas of the city.

"For the challenge." He sighed. "The difference between a made vampire and a natural one is that my siblings were created when one of my parents turned them from being a human. I was born into the family—grown in my mother's womb. My brothers and sisters aren't full-blooded siblings, and they know that. In the hierarchy of the family as it currently stands, I will always be above them. I was always the heir to my father's reign, always destined to be vampire king after him, but Sebastian would like to be in my position. He likely won't make a formal challenge to my position, but if he thinks he can ascend the easy way, he'll probably take it."

Nicolas spoke as if a weight had been lifted from him now that I knew his secret. He was more open, more approachable. More…*human.* Some of the shadows he seemed to draw around himself were no longer there.

"So if your parents were running around creating vampires…" I almost didn't have the courage to finish my question as I took in his raised eyebrow, but after fangs and glowing eyes, how much damage could an eyebrow really do? "Have you ever made a vampire?"

Even though I'd asked, his quick nod of affirmation surprised me. "Once."

"But I've just watched you drink a bag of blood. How could you make a vampire? That seems a bit like a vegetarian killing and butchering a cow."

He chuckled uneasily. "I'm not sure Jason would see it like that."

"*Jason?*" My voice came out as a high squeak.

Nicolas nodded. "Think of it as a mercy turn. Jason was dying, and I was the only one who could help him."

I made an effort to close my gaping mouth. But what the actual fuck?

"Let me get this straight." I sat taller in my seat. "You decided that the absolute safest person you could think of to guard me in your house was an actual vampire?" I'd watched movies with Jason, spent time with him. "He could have killed me!"

Nicolas shook his head. "He wouldn't dare. I am his sire—he wouldn't disobey or displease me."

I nodded. His imperious attitude amused me, but I didn't believe a word he said. "So you could magically stop a vampire attack in your house when you're at work in your casino? That sounds likely."

Nicolas growled low, the sound of frustration playing over my nerves and starting an ache in my core. I crossed my legs.

"I don't think you quite understand," he muttered. "This is my house. I'm the boss. I'm the first word and the last word, and my staff obey me. Jason most of all."

"Your *staff?*" My mouth hung open again, and this time I didn't bother to clack my teeth closed. "What do you mean, *your staff?*" But I didn't need him to answer. I already knew what he was about to say, and I started shaking my head even as he nodded his.

"All my staff are vampires." A fleeting smile played across his face, and I resisted the impulse to touch his cheek and press my mouth to his to capture that amusement. "I don't tolerate humans well. My staff is a loyal group, and they've been with me many years."

I patted my neck almost like I was searching for sore spots or bite marks. "But I could have been killed at any time. Mr. Baldwin could have gone crazy and ripped my throat out!" But even as I spoke the words, they sounded ridiculous.

Nicolas took them at face value, though. "I assure you, Baldwin would never do something so improper to a guest."

I closed my eyes. This was all so crazy. A house full of vampires, and I hadn't known a thing. "Wait a minute… The casino?"

Nicolas nodded. "Yes."

"There too? Oh my God. What is this? A hostile takeover, or something?"

He propped an ankle on his knee, the posture casual as he fiddled with the mug that was probably empty by now. "Hardly a takeover when we were here first, don't you think?"

Damn. I had to concede that point.

"Okay." I rubbed the back of my neck. "Okay, but I don't understand then. If you're all vampires here, and you're all vampires at the casino, then I assume you were all vampires at your family's party, too?"

He nodded affirmation again but didn't speak as he watched me. Maybe he knew I was trying to work something out.

"So I don't get why you need me. I saw your friend and heard what she said about being your mate, which I think must be like a vampire girlfriend." I glanced at him again, and his jaw tightened. Not acknowledgement of my assumption being correct, but not negation, either. "And if that's the case, I don't understand why I'm here. You've just told me you don't play well with humans…" I grinned. "Although with the length of your fangs, I can't imagine why."

My words came out more suggestive than the tease I'd intended, and he inhaled sharply as his eyes flashed red. I hurried on.

"I guess I just don't understand why you'd need me for events… And—" A thought occurred to me. "Was I ever in danger while I've been with you? Sometime not at the party?"

"Once." His answer was hoarse, his eyes haunted. "But I sorted it. The threat is neutralized. With me is the safest place you can be. Never wander away, never move from where I tell you to stay. I will *always* protect you, Leia."

"But I really don't understand." My tone verged on desperate. "I don't understand what's going on. Being a casino owner's arm candy was strange enough, but I was willing to do it for all that you offered me. But you're a vampire. You don't need me, so why am I here?" I took a deep breath and met his gaze. "What could a vampire possibly need with me?"

Chapter 18 - Nic

I sucked in a sudden breath I didn't know I'd needed, and it wedged in my chest like something sharp. As soon as Leia started asking questions, I should have known where this was headed.

I'd been stupid to think I could sit around being honest without it coming back to bite me. I should have just shut the conversation down, taken what I wanted, turned her for her own protection. Forget my own selfish requirements for my full ascension and reign. I could still fucking rule…it just wouldn't be the same for either of us if I didn't come into my full powers.

And I needed my full powers to truly be the male worthy of Leia. My head pounded, and I considered another mug of blood. But it tasted even worse than usual with Leia sitting across from me, her scent teasing me every time she moved.

I upended the mug and drained the dregs of my drink, ignoring the gritty texture of the last mouthful. Then I stood and walked to the small stainless sink in the corner, buying myself time as I washed the mug rather than simply rinsing it. I dried it, too, and selected the exact perfect spot in the cupboard where it should sit until I needed it again.

All that time, Leia didn't speak. She barely even seemed to breathe. She just waited. And usually, I excelled at a game of chicken. I was a patient man. I played the odds. The house *always* fucking won.

Always.

But I'd never played this game. And not with so much on the line.

I was about to fucking reveal my hand.

I'd planned to keep my distance and lay everything out carefully, concisely, matter-of-factly. But as I turned and looked at Leia, I couldn't. I couldn't stay away, I couldn't be detached.

It was all too important to be clinical and scientific. And Leia was more to me than that.

I sat next to her, probably taking up more room than I needed, and reached for her hands. She didn't resist, but there was no encouraging curl of her fingers around mine, either. I lifted her hand to my cheek, nuzzling it a little before I pressed a kiss to her skin, my gaze never leaving hers as I did.

Her cheeks pinked, and hope hammered my heart. She still reacted to my touch.

"Leia..."

She lifted an eyebrow. "A *Leia* moment? Must be important."

I kissed her hand again. "You're Leia, and I'm Nic."

Her lips parted, and I wanted to kiss them, but I needed to tell her our story first.

"And I know that's who we are, the only thing that matters, because...you're my true mate." I swallowed, seeking the words to make it plainer. "My bride."

She flinched a little, and I reflexively tightened my grip and pressed her palm to my cheek, unwilling to lose her or let her slip away. I watched her to make sure she was okay. I didn't want to hurt her. I just wanted to hold her close to me a little while longer while I explained everything.

"I need a bride, a virgin bride—"

She gasped.

"Don't worry. I've always known. I can tell."

"But how?" He cheeks darkened further.

I shrugged. "It's a difference in your scent."

A difference that aroused me more than I could describe. My gums itched, and I swallowed, trying to focus on something else that wouldn't make my fangs think it was time to come out to play.

"I smell?" She nearly drew away, but I shook my head.

"I don't mean it like that. Your scent is like a beacon for me. For all vampires. You're a siren, calling us all to our doom." I chuckled, the sound oddly self-conscious. "And I've never desired someone more in my whole life."

"Oh." The word was mostly silent as her eyes went wide. "But do all vampires want me like that?"

I nodded but changed my mind, ending on a shake. "Yes and no. No other vampire will want you more than I do because you're my true mate. No one else can claim that."

"True mate?" She swayed a little. "I thought the vampire shit was big news, but now you're saying things I don't really understand."

I drew a deep breath. This was the hard part. "In order to complete the ascension to my throne like I should, with the full respect of my people, my right to rule confirmed completely and to avoid challenge… I need to claim you. As a virgin, you can cement my right to rule." I paused to let that part sink in a little. "But as my true mate, my soul's other half, you alone can elevate my rule by increasing my powers beyond what they are now."

"Your powers?" She withdrew her hand from my cheek, and I let her go.

"Yes. Vampires naturally have increased strength, healing, speed, and also the power of compulsion. With you willingly by my side as my bride and my mate, my ability to command all of these things would be increased even further. I'd become truly the most powerful among my species."

"Willingly by your side?" She seemed to have lost the power to think of full questions and was just repeating things I'd said.

I wanted to reach for her and cradle her against my chest, but I resisted the urge. Crowding her seemed like a bad idea. "Yes. If we were to exchange blood, if you agreed and gave yourself to me willingly—"

She stood, her hands out like I'd advanced toward her. "But you said you don't take from the vein. I heard you say those words, Nicolas."

"Nic." My voice was soft, but I wanted nothing more than to hear her refer to me with that intimacy. As my mate, it was her right.

She shook her head, her denial clear. "*Mr. Dupont.* Don't think I don't remember you saying you don't take from the vein."

My chest ached as she sneered my name so formally. I wanted to stand and wrap my arms around her, to comfort myself more than her, but I didn't want to scare her. "I'd take from the vein for you."

She backed away. "Sounds like you benefit from that a whole helluva lot more than I do. Where would you keep me? Do I get my own fridge in your little blood room?" She gestured around as she spoke.

"As my claimed mate, you would benefit from increased protection from other vampires. No one would be able to hurt you again. It is the safest I can keep you."

But she wasn't listening. She was still taking small backward steps to the door, her arms out, warding me off. "Our contract was for a *month*." Her eyes blazed. "Just one month and then I'd be free forever, with my house, my bar, and hopefully a dad who isn't an addict. That was what I agreed to, what I signed up for, and now you're acting like this thing is a forever deal."

I stood, making the movement slow as she took a breath.

"I can't be your *mate*. That's a fucking ridiculous thing for you to say. We don't even know each other, and we don't have a relationship, no matter how hot you are!" She stopped abruptly, her chest heaving with deep breaths as she fought to control herself.

I'd just dumped a lot of information on her. I would have done this so much more gently if I'd been given the chance. But when I found her in here I...I had no choice.

"But you do think I'm attractive?" My gums ached again as pleasure spread through my chest. I stepped toward her, my hand out. "I can offer you anything your heart desires. All of the things we agreed to—your home, your bar, ongoing help for your father. At my side, you could have anything you've ever wanted, forever."

She froze, not even blinking.

"But it must be by my side." I lowered my voice. "Because I can't rule without you."

Her breaths were shallow, and I could almost see her brain cranking, so whatever I'd offered her must have been an interesting prospect.

"I can make you a very powerful woman," I said. "And you'd be safe."

She shook her head. "Don't be so fucking ridiculous. How could I ever be safe living among vampires?" She looked pointedly at the fridges. "I just watched you drink *blood*, and you've admitted that you want to drink *mine*. I don't know why you think that's safe—and I don't know why you think I'd even consider it."

"The mate bond would keep you safe. *I* would keep you safe. You belong to me." There was no reason for her to resist. I could give her everything she'd ever wanted and keep her safe from harm. "At my side, you'd never want or fear again."

She flung the door open. "No, Nicolas. This isn't what I signed up for, and I don't belong to anyone." Her words caught on a sob as she whirled from the room and slammed the door behind her, leaving only silence in her wake.

I sank onto the loveseat, regret leaving me hollow. I'd handled that all wrong, and I didn't know how to fix it. Leia was really angry, and I'd lost any of the trust and maybe even the mutual attraction that had been building between us.

If I chased after her now, it would likely make things even worse. I'd prove everything she thought she knew about vampires being predators and scary.

I looked at the closed door like I was trying to see through it, because if I couldn't fix this—if I lost her—I didn't know what I'd do.

Chapter 19 - Leia

Holy shit. Holy shit. My heart thumped wildly like it would crack a rib or two. Holy, holy shit.

Vampires.

What in the hell?

Stupid, fucking vampires didn't even exist.

Right?

Right? I mean, sure they didn't. Except now Nicolas wanted me to believe I'd been staying in a house full of them. I had to get out and get home somehow. But how? Mr. Jenkins was the driver, and Mr. Baldwin seemed to hang around just to open and close the fucking front door.

I sucked in a breath as I ran from the west wing with far less stealth than I'd used to enter. I wanted to lock the doors to the east wing behind me, but I didn't have a key, and hadn't Nicolas boasted of super strength or something equally as stupid? A locked door couldn't exactly keep him out of areas of his own home, either.

I hurried into my room. Surely Nicolas Dupont had broken his fucking contract now. Not declaring actual vampirism was pretty bad. And if not vampirism, insanity, which might have been worse.

Maybe my trip to his secret quarters had been worth it—it had yielded the results I wanted. Even if I could barely see through unwanted tears. Why the hell was I even crying? I brushed the tears from my cheeks and dragged my bag from where I'd left it in the stupidly big closet.

I'd be glad to get back to my own, cold home with normal sized spaces. Well, more normal than this house—the one Nicolas Dupont seemed to think could be everything I wanted.

Where did he get off trying to buy me?

Worse, I'd been so close to just giving him everything he wanted. Surrendering my kisses and opening my legs wide. I nearly gave the blood freak an all-access pass because I thought he'd liked me, and he made me feel incredible.

Even now, the memory of his touch sent a shower of sparks skittering through me.

I shoved only the clothes I'd brought with me in the bag. I didn't want any of the things Nicolas had bought. I didn't trust his motives anymore. I wasn't his bride. It sounded like every clichéd horror movie ever written, and there was only a short leap between being a vampire's bride and being Frankenstein's bride, and both of those things were like something out of a bad paranormal romance novel.

No one met a guy and married him inside a month.

No one.

But fresh tears welled in my eyes, and I ground them away with my fists. I had no reason to be so upset.

But hell. Bloody, fucking hell. The only cliché here was me. I'd started falling for Nicolas Dupont the moment he kissed me outside that grocery store, before I'd even known his name. I'd always been a sucker—ha!—for a mystery guy. A guy with a little bit of bad in him. Or a guy with a lot of bad in him. I wanted to be the center of someone's world. The sun he orbited around, and while he'd been plying me with gifts, Nicolas had made me feel that way.

Except now I knew why.

He *needed* me. And not because he actually would raze the world for one last kiss, but because I could bring him power.

And that was shit.

I needed to put as much distance between us as possible. And I almost didn't care if he walked our contract back because at least I wouldn't be beholden to the guy. I'd be able to look around and know I'd tried, but at least I wouldn't have anything that wasn't truly mine. I wouldn't still be taking part in the biggest bribe in Baton Rouge. Or was it blackmail? Maybe the name I put on Nicolas's game didn't matter.

His house wouldn't win this time.

I blew out a sigh. *Mom.* But she wouldn't have wanted this for me either. I couldn't settle on a life of being a walking, talking blood bag for a self-declared vampire king.

I took a final look around the bedroom. Damn, it really was a nice room.

Nothing more than a gilded cage for a one-month bride, though.

I dragged my phone from one of the pockets in my bag and scrolled through the stored list of phone numbers before settling on the number of a local cab firm run by one of Harry's old friends. They'd make sure I got anywhere I needed to go with no awkward questions and probably no expectation of payment, although if I could get to the bar, I could get to the till.

Hopefully takings had been steady.

I wavered as I stood behind the closed door, still in the opulent bedroom, somehow unwilling to take the next step to leave. Despite everything, I felt safe here.

I felt fucking *wanted*.

I had an undeniable pull to Nicolas. I'd let him touch me, and his fingers had been magic, his kisses like a drug created just for me. I wanted him to do more to me. In this bed.

In *his*.

A shudder ran through me, chasing a spike of desire at the idea of being surrounded by his scent, wrapped in his sheets, filled by his body.

A hunger like I'd never known threatened to claim me, and I took a deep breath then swallowed, forcing the hunger away.

Something about this man made me weak, and I couldn't afford to be weak. Steeling myself against the ridiculous, clearly self-destructive instinct to stay, I wrenched the bedroom door open and stepped out into the hallway.

Like the first night I'd arrived, Nicolas detached himself from the shadows, straightening from where he'd been leaning against the wall.

"Leia." His voice was hoarse.

"I have to go." I'd meant to sound firm and businesslike, but my words were desperate and sorrowful instead.

"Don't go." His eyes beseeched me, and when he walked toward me, I was powerless to escape.

My back hit the wall, and his arms braced either side me, pinning me there. Trapping me in another gilded cage, but I melted against him as he stared at me, one of his hands tangled loosely in my hair.

"Don't go," he said again. "Stay here—be mine."

"Nic." I stared at his mouth as he spoke, watching his lips form the words until I couldn't stand it anymore, and my body betrayed all of my logical decisions.

I rose on my tiptoes and my mouth brushed his. For a moment, his gray eyes darkened, clouds of confusion swirling in their depths. Then his gaze cleared, and he crushed me to him, aligning me to his body so I could feel every muscle and the evidence of his arousal laying heavy against my hip as he claimed my mouth, the force of his lips almost bruising as desperation flared between us.

His tongue slid against mine, probing forward before his movements became gentle and exploratory, almost languid in the most intimate of caresses.

My breathing spiraled out of control until I had to draw away to inhale. Nicolas's forehead rested against mine, his eyes closed so I couldn't see what he was thinking, didn't know how he felt.

"I have to go," I whispered, and his eyes sprang open, pain flaring dark red in the midst of all the gray.

"Stay." His word was nothing more than a breath. "I can give you anything you want."

But as he spoke those words, the certainty that he was wrong settled in my gut. I wanted to be *loved*, not just be required as the battery to supercharge whatever vampiric powers Nicolas thought he had.

"I don't just exist to secure your ascension to your father's throne." I tried to erase all regret from the words, but I wasn't sure I managed. "I won't."

He stepped back, his face paler than I'd seen it, and I took the opportunity to walk away from him, my steps silent as I moved down the hallway to the stairs.

For once, Mr. Baldwin was nowhere to be seen, but the taxi I'd requested idled outside the front door. I slid into the backseat and closed my eyes against the pain that streaked through my chest.

A sob lodged there, and before it grew and I couldn't speak around it, I forced out the address of The Pour House, my throat already thick, my eyes gritty. The driver met my gaze briefly in the mirror, his pale blue eyes kind as he nodded.

As he pulled away, I glanced out the back window, and that was a huge mistake. Nicolas stood in front of his house, watching me depart, his face twisted in something that looked far too much like anguish.

I curled my fists, pressing my nails into my palms to try to reawaken my resolve, thankful for the fact I still couldn't speak and tell the driver to turn around. I closed my eyes as I turned away so I didn't have to see Nicolas anymore, and a tear slid silently down the side of my nose as the car turned onto the road and we picked up speed as I left the impossible casino owner behind.

After we drew up at the bar, I dragged my small bag with me as I slid from the seat, and when I turned to tell the driver to wait while I found some money, he waved me away and drove off, leaving me standing outside my bar with nowhere to go but in.

I turned around and looked at it for a moment. Then I blinked and looked again. What the…? Tired, cracked paint had been replaced, and I had a brand new, updated sign. Tables and chairs sat outside on a refurbished covered deck, and they were full. Customers talked and laughed as low-volume Zydeco music filtered through state-of-the-art speakers.

I dropped my bag, and a puff of dry dust blew up from the ground. Surely this wasn't my place. My bar had never hopped or popped, or whatever shit bars were supposed to do. I'd limped from open to close, till count to till count, day after day, never sure if I'd be able to keep the lights on and the beer flowing, and now look at it.

The Pour House was open for business.

Holy shit.

I walked up sturdy steps to the raised deck and through the front door to be met by an icy blast of AC. For so long, I'd been used to little more than the bastard swamp cooler blowing out the laziest of breaths and a permanent sheen of sweat on my forehead and upper lip.

A server bustled by, a tray of food and drinks held expertly in one hand, a folded tray stand in the other, and I stepped back as a riot of sound, scent, and color invaded my senses. My bar was filled with chatter and laughter, and somewhere I could hear the dull clack of pool balls. And food. Holy hell, my stomach rumbled at the scent of seafood and deep-fried treats.

More music played in here but none of the noises competed. They just mingled into a general feel of happiness, and I blinked away yet more tears.

I automatically looked across the bar to Harry and Pierre's booth, and despite all of the changes, they were still there, steady and dependable as ever, big smiles on their faces as they chatted back and forth.

"Leia?"

I turned at the surprised voice, and Benedict immediately pulled me into a fierce hug like we were long lost friends. "What are you doing here? I didn't expect you back so soon," he murmured into my hair. Then before he gave me chance to answer, he released me, one arm still thrown over my shoulder as he gestured around. "What do you think of the place so far?"

"I... *So far?*" There was already so much.

"Well, yeah. I've barely started. You've been gone what...a few days?" He curled his lip slightly, then grinned. "And here you are already, ruining my surprise. I should've warned Nic he wouldn't be able to contain you for long."

"Holy shit... What have you been doing? Having guys working through the night?" I shook my head. "Don't answer that."

After everything Nicolas had told me about super strength and super speed, this made more sense than it should have.

I glanced at Benedict. Was he also…? No. I didn't want to know. This was too good to be true, and something in my life needed to absolutely stay that way.

Except.

Shit. I didn't even know if this place was still mine. I'd run away from the deal.

But Nicolas had done all of this for me to come home to. If I'd held out for the entire month, I would have come home to this and more, if Benedict said he still wasn't finished.

Except.

Who was I kidding? This had never been about a *month*. That was just one of Nicolas's lies. He hadn't done any of this for me. It was all for *him*. A carrot to dangle in front of me so I'd be the good little blood bag he needed.

Another weapon dangling from his utility belt.

Benedict glanced at me like he'd sensed my sudden shift in mood. "You okay?"

It gnawed in my gut that my bar was now everything I'd ever wanted it to be…but Nicolas had done all of this to get me to behave the way he wanted me to. It was the worst kind of manipulation. But I forced my mouth into a grin as I pushed Nicolas and his lies and deceptions to the back of my mind. "Sure. Am I welcome behind the bar?"

"Anytime." Benedict's smile made up for the grimace I was sure I'd just given him by arriving unannounced. "Wait until you see the new electronic ordering system. But first, I have to show you the kitchen. It's Chef's pride and joy."

"Chef's here?" I glanced toward the kitchen, beignets on my mind.

Benedict laughed, his deep chuckle a balm to so many of my aches. "Not right now, but he was very insistent about kitchen layout and also the dishes for the menu. I think we might actually have his secret recipe for gumbo." Benedict winked, and my heart twisted.

No matter Nicolas's ulterior motives, I didn't think Chef shared them. He, at least, had done this for *me*.

When my chest tightened again and my eyes itched, I stepped behind the bar. "Come on then, show me what this place can do."

I worked until closing, until I was almost dead on my feet, serving customers and chatting to Harry and Pierre, learning all of the new food, and it was a lot to take in. Benedict had streamlined the ordering system and cut new deals with suppliers, and now I seemed to have people lining up to extend credit for craft beers and wholesale food.

After the last customer left, and the AC was still refreshingly on, I turned to him. "How did you manage all of this?"

For a moment, I thought his eyes gleamed red, but then he leaned forward and turned off the neon sign behind the bar, and the effect disappeared. "I can be very persuasive."

I nodded, acknowledging his words, but I didn't pursue them or ask any other questions. There were probably things I didn't want to confirm about Benedict, too.

"I'm going to head home, I think. I'll be back at opening time tomorrow." I grabbed my bag and slung it over my shoulder, my phone already in my hand to dial the same taxi firm that brought me here. I even had some money in my pocket now.

"Oh, I can give you a ride, if you like? I need to see Nic up at his place, anyway." Benedict grabbed some keys from behind the bar.

"Uh..." Well, this was more awkward than I'd anticipated. "I'm no longer staying there. I'm going *home* home."

To his credit, Benedict merely raised an eyebrow, and that was the extent of his curiosity. He didn't even look like he was about to ask anything—although he could probably get any information he wanted directly from Nicolas if he was headed there to see him. But I couldn't worry about any gossiping the men did. I needed to get home and work out how I could hang on to the bar and the house. There had to be a way.

Even if Nicolas only let me work here until I figured it out.

I headed to the door then turned around. "How's my dad doing?"

Benedict nodded like he'd expected the question. "So far so good, but it's early days."

I withheld my sigh. Hopefully I hadn't fucked up my dad's chance of recovery, too. "I'll see you tomorrow."

Benedict offered me a wave and concerned eyes as I slipped out into the still-humid night.

The cab didn't take long to arrive, and my adrenaline and weird buzz faded as I sat in the back. Suddenly, I was just exhausted. I wanted to curl up under my thin blankets and sleep for a week. I didn't need cable TV after all. Just solitude and safety.

I was barely holding my eyes open against the gentle rhythm of the car and the road noise, but when we turned down my driveway, I automatically braced for the rough, jolting ride over the potholes and cracks. But nothing happened. We continued smooth as silk. I leaned forward to tap the driver's shoulder and tell him he'd taken a wrong turn.

I'd been bumping over my driveway for years—permanent bruise on my ass to prove it—each rut familiar, and we were definitely headed to the wrong house.

My theory was confirmed when the driver let out a low whistle. "Having some work done, cher?"

"What? No." I leaned forward and squinted into the darkness, gasping as the cab's headlights picked up the gleam of metal in front of my house. "What the…?"

The moment the cab stopped, I leaped out and turned my face up, taking in the scaffolding stretching into the sky around the front of my house.

The cab driver got out, too. "This is going to be beautiful when it's done." He looked at me. "Back to its former glory?"

"It just might be." My head spun as I looked at a façade that used to be cracked and dirty that was now smooth and gleaming bright white in the soft moonlight as I dug some cash out of my pocket and held it out to him.

He shook his head. "Looks like you have more important things to spend your money on, cher."

I walked to the front door, and he waited for me to open it before he drove away, leaving me to watch his red taillights recede down the driveway.

Well, shit. First The Pour House and now my actual house? It was all too much. What the hell was Nicolas up to?

I stepped into the entrance hall and my first breath was of pure fresh paint. In fact, paint so fresh, I could taste it. My hand automatically found the light switch, and I lit the darkness, chasing the shadows away with more than the usual pale-yellow glow.

A chandelier dripping crystal beads hung from the tall ceiling and cast rainbows on the tops of the walls, and the hardwood floor, newly polished, gleamed beneath my feet. I hardly dared walk on it as I headed into the living room, where my feet sank into plush new carpet. When I switched the light on, all I could see was the huge portrait of my parents and me above the refurbished fireplace. Mom's smile was beautiful as she looked out at me as if she approved of the changes that were taking place, and I could almost feel her presence.

"Oh, Mom," I whispered. "I think I might have fucked up."

Up until this moment, I'd been able to tell myself Nicolas was acting solely in his own self-interest, but that didn't explain why he'd displayed my family so prominently in my house for me, and why he'd gone to all this trouble.

If he'd intended only to keep me, and for me to never return here or to The Pour House, why? This was more than protecting an investment, more than simply refurbishing a house to sell. He'd turned it back into my home, and a home meant to appeal only to one person—me.

Like I mattered.

To him.

Shit. I sank onto the sofa and looked up at Mom's photo. She continued to smile at me, her joy never wavering, but guilt weighed heavily on me as I looked around my house.

The improvements looked as though they were all being made with me in mind, and I didn't know who'd been consulted, but there were even new DVDs in a seemingly random stack on the table, most of them ones Jason and I had laughed over.

Someone cared.

And now I was here all alone. Alone and wondering if I'd gotten everything wrong.

Almost too tired to think, I dragged myself from the sofa and trudged up the stairs to my room.

I stopped in the doorway, remorse chasing away my initial delight as I stared at my room. Once again, someone had perfected my space, only this looked a hell of a lot like the ruined room in Nicolas's home must have looked before it was torn apart. Sumptuous fabrics graced a new four-poster bed, and it was a room fit for a bride.

Apparently, Nicolas thought it was fit for me.

Chapter 20 - Nicolas

I shoved my paperwork to one side, the movement frustrated and rough. Things had all gone to fucking shit. I'd called for the paperwork of more of my biggest debtors, but it turned out that none owed me as much as Jean Boucher had, and none would provide me with anything of the same worth in return.

I growled and pushed the paperwork from my desk completely, watching it scatter uselessly to the floor. Then I stood and wandered to the mirrored glass overlooking my casino before resting my forearm on the window as I watched people I had no respect for literally gift their money to me.

Fucking humans.

Stupid species.

No common sense. No wonder I couldn't stand them.

I couldn't hear the game floors from here—the rooms were insulated against even my super-hearing—but I could imagine the sound of the chips, and farther away, the chimes of the slots.

The entrance door opened to admit another lamb to my slaughter, and for a moment, my heart froze in my chest as I took in dark brown hair and a slender frame. But it wasn't her, and I looked away again.

"Everything okay in here?"

I jerked at Jason's voice, distracted by too much noise in my head, and that was dangerous. "Why wouldn't it be?" My words came out terse and biting. I half-turned to glance over my shoulder as I waited for his reply.

He gestured to the paperwork on the floor. "You dropped something."

"Fuck it." I returned to watching the casino, this time tuned in to the rustle of Jason's pants as he crouched and began to shuffle the paperwork back into order. Each slice of the papers being piled together cut a fine line of irritation across my skin. "Leave it."

"But I can get some of the others onto these collections."

I waved a hand. I didn't care anyway.

He sighed, and I could feel his gaze—his damn curious gaze, probably filled with concern if I knew Jason—on the back of my head. "What can I do?" His voice was no louder than a murmur, ensuring any vampire who happened to be passing my door wouldn't hear.

"Nothing." I sighed. "There's nothing to do. Collect the debts, bring in the money. It's business as usual."

"And what about not-business?" he prodded. "What about pleasure?"

I barked out a laugh as some dumb guy below me gave in to a premature celebration over a win he hadn't yet made. *I* was that fucking dumb guy. So close and everything had slipped away. "Pleasure's overrated."

"But you *had* slipped into pleasure then?"

Too late, I realized my mistake. I'd said too much and not denied Jason's words. I'd shown him my hand. I said nothing further.

"Nic?" Jason prompted.

"What?" Usually my bad-tempered attitude made even him leave, but not this time.

"The house always wins, Nic. So where is Leia?"

I sighed. "The house didn't win this time."

Jason snorted laughter and tapped the files against my desk like he was straightening them. "Then change that. I've never known you to accept a loss with anything like good grace. You're always biding your time, always watching to reel the punter back in."

I sighed, so soft I hoped he didn't hear it. Leia was more than a punter.

"You can't pretend Leia wasn't important, or that her whole family wasn't important. Are you just going to let everything end like this? She's across town, not in another country, not dead."

Shit. So close. She was so fucking close. I closed my eyes against the people chancing their luck in La Petite Mort.

"Well?"

I spun around. "Shit, Jason. For fuck's sake. What's gotten into you? Can't you just leave it?"

But he stood his ground, holding the files he'd collected against his chest. "No. No, I can't, and neither should you. I've never seen you like you were with Leia."

"Yeah?" I forced a cruel smile. "I'll find another virgin. That's all I need to rule."

He scoffed and shook his head. "Yeah. You just keep telling yourself that, Nic. Keep telling yourself that one day you'll find another virgin and she'll be enough. Keep telling yourself that next time you meet Leia Boucher *and she's no longer a virgin* that discovery won't kill what's left of your decaying, blood-bag guzzling heart."

"Get out." I kept my order calm and controlled as I pointed to the door like Jason didn't know where it was.

He shrugged. "I figure if I don't tell you, no one else will. Who else here dares to say what you need to hear?"

"What makes you think I need to hear it?" My eyes narrowed and my heart rate accelerated— signs I was about to become dangerous, but my sireling didn't even flinch.

"Because sometimes, Nic, you're stubborn. You're stubborn and you're stupid and you're old and self-defeating. And you forget that the house always wins only because you make it that way. So why have you stopped playing this game? Why have you thrown in your hand?"

"She left me." And there it was. The bald truth, the source of my pain.

"So she injured your pride?"

"Yes." But that was a lie.

Leia had been many things. She was a virgin with virgin blood—never known a man to claim her with his cock nor a vampire with his fangs— she had a strong ancestry via her matriarchal line, and she was beautiful. Added to that, she alone could increase my power. She was my true mate. In short, she would make the ultimate bride.

But I hadn't expected to see this as anything but another game I could win. It was the culmination of a business transaction, turning in my chips for my reward.

I hadn't expected to fucking care for her, and now there was a hole in my chest like she'd ripped my heart out and packed it in her bag with whatever else she'd chosen to take. That was unfair, though. She'd taken only what she'd brought. She'd very carefully left all of my gifts to her behind.

Which didn't explain my heart. The one thing I hadn't intended to give her and she'd taken anyway.

She'd veered between fear and fury before she left, but despite that, she'd still desired me.

"I can't let her go." I spoke the words quietly, but they were like some kind of grand realization.

"That's more like it." Jason sounded satisfied behind me, and I'd forgotten he was there again.

Fucking humans and fucking sirelings.

At least she was safe. Benedict had already been to see me and told me all about his surprise visitor. And I was heading out to The Pour House later this evening to see what Benedict had done to the place so far.

If Leia happened to be there when I showed up, well, so be it. I loved a good coincidence.

I left my office early, quietly, almost sneaking out. I called my own hours, but they were always longer than anyone else's. Only not today.

Jenkins met me downstairs and then we were off, my nose full of Leia's scent where the back seat of my car seemed to have absorbed it, my memories full of the warmth and welcome of her pussy as my fingers had conquered it. I yearned to taste it, to taste her, and almost growled as my cock jerked and my gums ached.

When Jenkins drew up at The Pour House, I didn't step out right away. Instead, I admired everything Ben had accomplished. There was a reason he was my trusted right hand, and circumstances like this one always proved me right.

I'd worked hard to surround myself with people I deemed loyal and trustworthy. I didn't give my friendship easily, but I meant it when I did. I gave my love even less easily, and the hole in my chest was proof as to why for that.

When Jenkins finally turned, his lips parted like he might ask a question, I moved to open the door.

"I don't think I'll be long," I said.

"Very good, sir."

I didn't really know how long I might be, but if I had to, I'd reemerge with Leia over one shoulder, my hand on her ass to keep her still, because she was *mine*. And I wasn't going to let her go this easily.

I paused outside the doors. Ben had truly accomplished a miracle. He'd taken Leia's bar from some hole-in-the-wall, rundown place to a popular spot, with a crowd big enough that I couldn't even start to guess where he'd collected them all from. They'd arrived so quickly, it didn't seem possible. Perhaps he'd compelled them.

But even that wouldn't matter. Crowds drew more crowds, and more crowds would fill Leia's cash register. And knowing Ben, he'd only gotten started.

I hadn't come here to stand outside the door, though, and as soon as I entered Ben looked up from where he was serving customers, his gaze meeting mine as he grinned.

"Nic." He shouted my name across the bar. "You the reason Leia hasn't shown up? You manage to convince her to come back to you?"

The grin I'd aimed at him in return slipped a little. Fuck. I couldn't be the all-conquering hero come to claim what was mine, not when what was mine wasn't even here. I almost turned to leave, but Ben gestured me over.

"Come and see what we've been doing with the place. Leia was really impressed."

I nodded, sure she had been. Ben had surpassed himself by introducing an old-style atmosphere that was friendly and welcoming—perfect for regulars and tourists alike, and maybe now tourists would make their way out here—especially if that was Chef's gumbo I smelled.

Ben grinned again as I joined him at the counter, and he handed me a beer. "Craft beer from a local microbrewery. No more supply problems." He winked. "Do you want to see the new ordering system? The kitchen? The sound system? Where shall we start?"

"What time's Leia due?" My clipped question sounded rude, but she was uppermost on my mind.

Where she was, what she'd say when she saw me, how she she'd taste, how her body would feel as I slid inside her.

Ben frowned and checked his watch. "She said opening, but maybe she changed her mind."

I matched his frown as I took a step backward, jostling a guy standing too close behind me. I hissed a little over my shoulder and he backed off.

"She should be here then." I directed my words at Ben.

"Maybe, but there are a lot of changes she might want to explore at the house, you know?"

I did know, and I doubted any of the changes overrode Leia's desire to see The Pour House be a success. I'd wanted to give her a taste of the luxury she could live in at my side, but after the way she left me, I doubted she was basking in anything I'd done to her home.

"You worried?" Ben handed the guy behind me a beer and waved his money away. "It's on my grumpy friend, here," he said as he indicated me. "An apology for his rudeness."

"Yeah, a little," I answered Ben's question as my stomach churned. It was still a foreign feeling, worry for someone else. Everyone I knew could look after themselves easily—especially in our territory.

But with Leia, my heart was walking around outside my body, completely unprotected.

"I think I'll head over to her place. See what she thinks of the changes." I checked behind me this time. I had no desire to buy all the new customers a drink.

"Not just changes. *Improvements*. And I'm sure she loves them." Ben didn't even falter in his rhythm as he held multiple conversations and served different people a variety of drinks.

I'd made the right choice in asking for his help with this.

Jenkins was sitting right where I'd left him, and I took my place behind him again.

"Leia's house, please."

He nodded, but I expanded anyway.

"She wasn't at the bar." It wasn't like me to talk unnecessarily, but something about Leia not being where she'd said she'd be made me nervous. And I didn't like being nervous any more than I liked being worried.

Jenkins ate up the miles like he knew I was in a hurry. He probably did. I didn't usually fidget. But I tapped my fingers against the door and shifted my position, alternately leaning forward to check the traffic and looking out the windows to check our location.

We turned onto Leia's driveway, and I tightened my grip on the door handle to prevent myself leaping from the car while it was still moving. I'd never felt desperation like it, and it coursed through my veins. I needed to see her and make sure she was okay.

"Wait here." I issued the gruff command as Jenkins finally stopped the car. Then I got out and knocked on Leia's door.

It swung open under my hand, and I caught my breath. Shit. The house was quiet. Silent, really, and I closed my eyes as I listened. The wards weren't even fucking in place yet. I'd arranged that for after all the work had been completed.

But it should have been safe.

A clock ticked somewhere, and something settled. A dripping tap and the hiss of water along a pipe... But nothing else.

No heartbeat, no breathing sounds.

I stepped inside. Leia's scent was strong, so she'd definitely been here. So had my men—working on the renovations. But that was the other issue with the silence. Where were the workers?

No one was here. But wait. No. I was wrong.

Like an undertone to the odor of the paint, there was a copper tang. Unfamiliar vampire, too, but that could be my work crew—I didn't know them. They just worked for me.

I followed the scent of blood, past knocked-over paint buckets and through rooms where all the lights were on, to three dead workmen. They lay in a pool of blood, their heads half hanging off, and their hearts had been ripped from their chests. This was overkill and then some.

My own heart knocked against my ribs, gathering speed as I pulled my phone from my pocket and increased my walking pace, almost blurring through the house.

"Leia!" Her name was a plea. Something desperate as I forced it from my lips.

I took the steps two at a time and only glanced at my phone as I scrolled to Jason's speed-dial.

"Nic?" He already knew something was wrong. Could probably feel it in our blood bond.

"She's not here." I gasped the words out. "She's...something's wrong."

I followed her scent to a closed door and swallowed my next words with an audible gulp.

There was no heartbeat in the house, at least three dead workers, and a closed bedroom door.

I closed my eyes briefly as I pushed the door open, not wanting to confront my worst fear. But it was okay. Her bedroom was empty, and the bed didn't even look slept in. A breath of relief whooshed from me.

"Nic? I'm on my way." Jason sounded distracted now like he was focused on another task. "I'm getting my gun from the safe."

"I'm at her house. She's not here." I started to turn around, but something lying on the comforter of the pristine bed caught my gaze. I stepped closer. "Fuck, *no*."

I picked up the note, and the paper rustled as I tightened my fingers. My chest tightened, and I couldn't draw a breath or push one out. My head pounded, and my stomach roiled as I fought to retain my last meal.

"Nic?" Jason seemed to have forgotten most of his other words.

"We've got a problem." I spoke through gritted teeth, and I didn't need to see my reflection to know my eyes glowed red as I focused on the note again:

Let the war begin.

I bellowed my rage into the bedroom I'd had created for Leia—a bride's room with no bride. Someone had taken what belonged to me.

But worse, they'd taken Leia.

My Leia.

War. Fuck, yes. Someone had my mate, and I'd win every battle in front of me to reclaim her.

I'd burn the whole world to ash if I needed to.

Chapter 21 - Leia

I groaned and rolled over, my head pounding. Music wove around me. A jazz trumpet, loud and far too happy. And the pounding inside my head was matched outside my head by the jarring beat of a large drum. I swallowed against a roil of nausea.

Voices cheered and people clapped somewhere farther away, and there was laughter, but my eyelids were too heavy to lift. Everything was foggy like someone had stirred my thoughts into a thick gloop.

I groaned, then retched and swallowed against the bile rising in my throat.

Something was wrong. Nothing sounded the same, nothing smelled the same. I'd left Nicolas's house and come home, but now I wasn't there either.

Panic sliced a keen cut of awareness through me. *Not at home.* I opened my eyes, but the sudden movement hurt and I closed them again even as fear began to take hold. It whispered across my skin, and I shuddered.

I rolled on my side and opened my eyes carefully. It was like I'd spent the night drinking, matching Dad mouthful for mouthful. The room spun, the walls looming in and out of focus as I tried to make sense of what I could see while the panic settled to a steady buzz that threatened to cloud my senses.

The walls were jarring, vivid splashes of color, and I closed my eyes again. I was definitely somewhere new, and… Fuck. Fuck, what did I remember? Why did everything hurt?

Shit. I needed to think. But my skull still beat to its own rhythm. I shifted onto my back and waited until the room had stopped swirling around me before I prayed for a plain white ceiling and opened my eyes.

When everything had finally steadied, I glanced around, taking my time with each movement as I cataloged my surroundings, trying to be logical and keep the terror clutching at my throat at bay. My chest had tightened, too, and my breaths were shallow.

Okay. Okay, I could do this. I'd just spent time with the Vampire King of Baton Rouge and survived his brother nearly biting me. I could find my way out of one small room. I swallowed, the movement awkward and heavy.

I was on a heavy wooden bed, and the only other things in the room were a window and a door. Well, that limited my possibilities for breaking the glass and making my escape.

I climbed from the bed, hesitance delaying each movement as I tested each one to see how much it might hurt. Finally, I leaned against the window, breathing heavily, although I couldn't say what had taken most of the effort. I felt all around it for a latch or a fastening, but there was nothing to use to open it. It was simply panes of glass set firmly within a frame. The glass wasn't even truly transparent. I couldn't see out and no one could properly see in.

No one would know I was even here.

A scream threatened to rip from me, but I held it in. Maybe the only weapon I currently had was my silence. My thoughts were fragmented, and I breathed deeply as I tried to bring them back into order.

Fear was my enemy. I needed to calm down.

I dragged myself to the door and turned the handle, but nothing happened. It didn't even rattle. Nothing groaned or creaked—maybe only my bones as a sigh rising through me shook them.

I waited a little. Silence was good, but not if it prevented being rescued.

"Hello?" My voice was scratchy, and I tried again a little louder, ignoring the instinct to make myself as small as possible and hide away.

The panic pressed harder now, heavy and cloying, and my breathing was increasingly rapid.

I pressed my ear to the door, but either the wood was too dense or there was nothing beyond it because all I heard was my own blood thrumming through my head.

I beat on the door until my hands were sore and I was so tired I wanted to fall back into the bed.

There was no way out, and all I could do was wait. But I didn't get back into the bed. I couldn't be lying there helpless if someone appeared, and someone would appear, I was certain about that much.

What was the last thing I remembered? I waded through my gloopy thoughts, searching for my memories. I'd left the bar and gone home, and Nicolas had made changes. Lots of changes.

My room had been different…but not like this. I saw my room, but did I fall asleep in it? I'd seen the bed but had no memory of lying down.

But who would take me? Who the hell would bring me here to this noisy, colorful place?

I groaned and pressed a finger to my left temple to try to ease the throbbing. I'd gone home, but maybe Nicolas had never released me from my contract. It had seemed easy. So easy.

Perhaps too easy.

Maybe he'd never let me go. Nicolas must have taken me. It was the only explanation. He knew exactly where I'd be. I'd run away from him, but he'd known I wouldn't run far.

Fucking Nicolas Dupont.

But the panic subsided a little. If Nicolas had taken me to fulfil the contract, I could at least handle that. I'd deal with him when I felt stronger. Decision made, I approached the bed and climbed back on.

I closed my eyes and prepared to sleep. Now I knew what had happened, I didn't care to stay awake. Nicolas could find out exactly how disinterested I was in his games.

I'd just relaxed when the door cracked like thunder as it smacked against the wall, and I almost fell off the bed.

"Nicolas Dupont," I yelled before I'd fully straightened. "What the hell do you think—"

I bit off my words.

Man in front of me.

Not Nicolas.

He grinned, then spoke like he could read my addled mind. "Oh, I'm not Nicolas Dupont, *ma chérie*." But something in the way he spoke Nicolas's name implied a viciousness not present in his casual pose or his easy grin.

My skin shifted like it wanted to crawl away from my body in this guy's presence. I lifted my chin, trying to prevent myself from shaking.

"Where am I?" My voice rang out clearly, despite the unwillingness of my skin to stay and protect me.

He laughed. "Why, New Orleans. Can't you tell? We're holding quite the party to celebrate your arrival."

He gestured vaguely toward the window, indicating outside, where the music continued.

There was even something sinister about his laugh. Something otherworldly that I couldn't pinpoint. He had an eerie calm, but his eyes were alive and alight, almost crazy.

"Is Nicolas here?" I tried to sound casual as I stepped farther behind the bed, almost shielding myself from this man I didn't know.

"*Is Nicolas here?*" He mimicked me, his voice falsetto, his hands clasped sweetly over his heart. Then his voice returned to normal. "No. He is not here. That would be quite unacceptable. He'd spoil all our fun."

He took one gliding step toward me, then another.

I stifled a scream.

Fucking hell. Another predatory male.

Except this one made me long to be anywhere but in his presence, while Nicolas's proximity had made me long for him inside me.

I shook my head, still trying to stir my thoughts into action. None of this made any sense. "What do you want? Why am I even here?" The heavy fear from before returned, binding me, constricting me.

He laughed again, the sound rolling over me and leaving me unclean. "I want to get everything I've always wanted. And you're the key to it all."

I opened my mouth to ask what the hell he meant, but still laughing, he began to back away, until all I could see and hear was his eyes watching me and his laugh booming off the walls like the sound itself could attack me.

He slammed the door shut behind him, and fine pieces of plaster flaked off the wall and floated to the floor, but it was like the laughter continued, mocking me. He'd left without even giving me a name, without telling me anything he planned to do with me.

Probably no one else even knew where I was.

Who would think to look?

Nicolas. The thought came to me unbidden, piercing through the fear.

But I knew, and with a certainty that shocked me. If anyone looked for me, it would be him.

If anyone came for me, it would be Nicolas Dupont.

More than once, he'd declared me as his, and if I believed anything of him at all, it was that he didn't stand idly by while someone took what was his away from him.

I ran to the door and beat on it again, then the window, a whirlwind of frenetic activity as I tried to find a way out, but the music continued, raucous and happy, and there was no way anyone near that noise would hear my pitiful attempts to get their attention.

None of this made sense. And I should never have run away from Nicolas. He'd begged me to stay. In his house, I might have been his pawn, a piece in his game to get what he wanted for his future—but here in this strange room with a man I'd never met, I was a victim, and for the first time since I'd signed Nicolas's contract, I was a true prisoner.

I might even be food.

Thank you for reading Taken by the Vampire King. We hope you enjoyed the start of Nic and Leia's story. Curious about Nic's next move? Order Stolen by the Vampire King now so you don't miss finding out what he does!

Made in the USA
Middletown, DE
21 September 2024